SEEKER'S WORLD

K. A. RILEY

For all the young people who sometimes feel invisible.

CONTENTS

ABOUT THE BOOK

"You are a Seeker.

Prove yourself worthy, and you may just save the world."

On her seventeenth birthday, Vega Sloane receives a strange and puzzling gift: a key in the shape of a dragon's head, along with a note that claims she's destined to save the world.

When the handsome and mysterious Callum Drake enters her life, she finds herself inextricably drawn to him, and more questions begin to arise. Who is the boy beyond the exquisite façade and charming smile? Is he an ally, or the very enemy she needs to fight off?

Vega soon discovers that she's being recruited to attend a magical Academy in a world beyond her own—a school where those known as the Blood-Born train and compete to see who comes out on top.

The only problem?

Everyone seems to want her dead.

Well, *almost* everyone.

PART I
FAIRHAVEN

BIRTHDAY

THE SOUND THAT JARRED ME AWAKE ON THE MORNING OF MY seventeenth birthday was a familiar girl's voice chirping, *"Hey, Vega! Pick up your damned phone! Hey, Vega! Vegaaaa!"*

A smile spread over my lips as I rolled over and reached for my cell phone, which was sitting on top of the half-read pile of novels on the white night stand next to my bed.

"Thanks again for recording the stellar personalized ringtone, Liv," I muttered as I clicked the reply button and pressed the phone to my ear. "You really know how to make a girl feel special."

"Happy Birthday, Vega!" she sang, deftly ignoring the mental arrows of sarcasm I was shooting her way. "May I remind you on this July twenty-sixth that you're now officially one year closer to your demise?"

"Yes, and thank you for *that*, too."

"You're welcome. But for the record, if you'd had the two weeks I've just had, you'd be praying for death."

I let out a snicker. "Let me guess: You didn't have the greatest time at the cottage with your parents."

Liv drew out a pathetic sigh, followed by a dramatic inhalation, which meant she was about to set off on a superhumanly fast verbal tirade. "Well, let's see. It rained for ten days straight. There was no internet and no cable TV. We lived like freaking cavemen. I'm talking jigsaw puzzles and board games, and not the fun kind with dirty words. We're talking full-on financial transactions and real estate deals. Not to mention that my dad cheats constantly. I pretty much tore out half my hair, and I'm now on the verge of a psychotic break. But hey, thanks so much for asking."

"I'm sorry for your ordeal," I said. "It reminds me of the stories of glassy-eyed soldiers coming back from war. I don't know how you survived."

"The worst part," Liv added without missing a beat, "is that I'm about to go on a ten-day road trip with the parental units. They want to leave tomorrow, and I've barely had time to recover from the cottage. You may as well just kill me now."

"I'd love to, but I hear they arrest people for stuff like that," I said, hoping she'd change the subject. The truth was, it was hard to hear Liv complain about her parents. I'd lost mine four years ago in a car accident, and the only immediate family I had left was my older brother Will. It was hard not to envy anyone who still had the luxury of spending time with their family.

"I'm sorry," Liv said, apparently picking up on my tone. "I'm being an inconsiderate ass."

"It's okay," I replied.

"No, it's not. Besides, the reason I called wasn't to moan about my life. I know it must suck to be alone today, so I'm hereby forcing you to hang out with me on this fine birthday morning. I'll be there in fifteen minutes."

"What?" I yelled, shooting up to a sitting position, "But I haven't even showered yet!"

"Fine. I don't want to hang out with you if you're rancid. Tell you what—it's ten now. I'll give you exactly half an hour, then we're going on an adventure."

"An adventure? In Fairhaven that doesn't mean much."

"You might be surprised," Liv said in an uncharacteristically cryptic tone. "I may not have an actual birthday present for you, but I do have a cunning plan that involves both your future happiness and your present pleasure."

"Um, I really don't like the sound of that," I replied with a yawn and a stretch. I could practically feel the mischievous smile in Liv's voice. This was her *I'm going to meddle in your life in ways that make you cringe* tone, one that had led to multiple disasters over the course of our teen years, normally involving some boy or another. If I was book-crazy, Liv was boy-crazy, and I've always been fairly sure she'd stack guys up on her nightstand and flip through them one at a time if she could.

Still, I was curious enough to kick the sheets off my feet and yank myself out of bed.

"Just...trust me," she said. "Or don't. Now go shower and make yourself presentable, Smellypants."

"Fine," I said in surrender and with what I think may have been the first ever audible eye-roll. "See you in half an hour."

"Bye, Stinkyface!"

"Bye, Bossybutt," I chuckled as I hung up.

Much as she could be overwhelming, I had to admit that I enjoyed having a take-charge best friend. While I fretted over every option and decision, Liv plowed through life like she was the offspring of a bulldozer and a wrecking ball.

She was my polar opposite. She was outgoing, bouncy, and fun. I was on permanent alert, always analyzing the possibilities, second guessing myself, and constantly on the lookout for danger around every corner. Meanwhile, Liv was completely lacking in self-consciousness. She was the only reason I ever actually went to parties or socialized with anyone—not that I did either very often. She was fearless, gregarious, perky...everything I was not.

Then again, I was everything *she* wasn't. I was competitive. I was focused. I'd always excelled at school and consistently maintained the highest grades among my peers at Plymouth High. I was also the fastest female sprinter in my grade. Which was a dubious honor, given that it was probably inspired by my innate desire to flee from other human beings.

My almost obsessive need to excel at school and track was something Liv had always found odd at best, repugnant at worst. Last year, over tea at the café across the street from our school, she asked me why I always tried so hard.

"It's not so much that I care about getting the best grades or winning or anything," I told her with a shrug. "It's just that I freaking *hate* losing."

Waving her hand in the air like she was scanning a newspaper headline, Liv said she could see my tombstone now: "Here lies Vega Sloane. Winning was more important to her than life itself. And that's why she's dead."

The truth, of course, was that I knew if I didn't excel at my classes, I'd fail to secure the scholarships I needed if I ever wanted to go to college. And without college, I'd probably end up living in a soggy, toxic cardboard box, licking discarded hamburger-wrappers in a desperate attempt to stave off starvation.

My older brother Will and I had been living on our own since our parents died, and we'd survived on a meager inheritance and his earnings ever since. Will, who was twenty-two now, had put off attending university during that time so he could pick up jobs here and there, always insisting I avoid part-time work while I was still in high school.

"Focus on your studies while you can," he always said. "You have plenty of time to work your butt off and be miserable later."

All the while, he'd kept us alive. He'd invested our small inheritance cleverly enough so we managed to keep our house and scrape by with the basic necessities. He sacrificed so much of his own life, all so I could lead a relatively normal teenage existence. I owed him everything, and, as I eased out of bed and slid my feet into my fuzzy-bunny slippers, I made a mental note to tell him so.

Will had been in Europe for most of July, but he was supposed to get home later in the afternoon to celebrate my birthday with me. Even though he only planned on staying for the night, his homecoming was the best gift I could possibly imagine.

Excited to see what the day would bring but slightly worried about what Liv had in store for me, I stretched my arms over my head as I walked by my open window, which overlooked the back yard and the thick canopy of trees making up the dense woods surrounding the dead-end street where I'd grown up, on the edge of our very small town.

A cool breeze was flitting in through the thin curtains, bringing with it the scent of damp grass and leaves. Though it was still weeks away, autumn already hung in the air. So strange to think that soon I'd be starting my last September of high school. By this time next year, I'd be heading off to college to study and meet new people...and probably coming up with excuses for why I couldn't go out and party with them.

After an all too quick shower, I raced back to my bedroom and threw on a pair of jeans, a gray t-shirt and hoodie. I yanked open my bedroom door and marched downstairs, pausing on the landing to tidy my long ringlets of curly, dark hair in the silver-framed mirror hanging on the forest green wall.

I wasn't generally a fan of mirrors, probably because I wasn't generally a fan of my face. I'd never liked my combination of prominent cheekbones and my hybrid complexion of orange and mocha freckles—thanks to my mother's Kenyan roots and my father's Irish skin, which was so pale my mother had always joked that just thinking about the sun turned him fire-engine red.

The thick, dark eyebrows arching over my oddly-large hazel eyes and my slightly pouty lips tended to make strangers think I was perpetually annoyed, which was fine with me. I considered it a natural defense, like the scales of a brightly-colored lizard or the jagged thorns of a pufferfish. "Come close and you'll regret it," my features said. It was what Liv called *Resting Screw-You Face*, but I suspected that was only because she didn't actually want to call me a bitch.

When I was little, my mother told me a thousand times how each of my perceived imperfections was really a mark of beauty, but I'd never treated her comments with anything other than skepticism. "It's your job to say stuff like that," I told her when I was twelve. "It's not like you'd say if I was hideous."

"Yes, but..." she'd replied. Then, when her argument had stopped dead in its tracks, she'd let the subject drop for a few months until she felt it was time to bring it up again.

Now, of course, I missed her words of motherly reassurance. I missed everything about her. Her face, her scent, the way she laughed every time my father told one of his terrible jokes.

I missed those terrible jokes, too.

As I scrutinized my reflection, I felt all of a sudden like I was staring at someone I'd never met. Maybe it was the way the morning light was hitting me, but for some reason my face seemed to have thinned out since yesterday, as though I'd magically managed to shed the last remnants of my nebulous childhood puffiness. My eyes looked brighter than usual, the green in my irises kicking it up a notch from their usual dull shade, like someone had turned on a light inside me.

Well, I supposed it made sense. The face staring back at me, I reminded myself, was now seventeen years old. Maybe it was the accelerating sprint toward adulthood that had altered me overnight. Or maybe it had been so long since I'd really bothered assessing myself that I'd forgotten what I really looked like.

With a deep exhalation, I plodded the rest of the way down the stairs. When I reached the foyer, I was greeted by the sight of a large yellow envelope sitting on the floor by the mail slot. I reached down and grabbed it, flipping it over.

The tidy handwriting read:

Miss Vega Sloane
12 Cardyn Lane
Fairhaven, MA

The return address indicated that the envelope had come from my father's mother, who lived in Cornwall, England. She sent me birthday cards every year. Usually they featured cutesy pictures of sparkly unicorns or prancing teddy bears, and pithy quotes like, "You're a magical squishy-wishy granddaughter!" or "Hugs to a very special girl who's about to turn moody and grow hair in strange and surprising places!"

Okay, so those weren't the exact words. But the end result of those *my-how-you've-grown* cards was usually profound mortification on my part.

So I was surprised when I tore the envelope open and pulled out this year's offering only to find an eerily dark painting on the cover of the bleak card.

The image was of a foreboding forest path. A series of spindly trees stretched out over it, their branches looming like deadly talons above the overgrown walkway. Far in the distance at the trail's end was a mysterious source of light that looked even more terrifying than the trees themselves. I couldn't help but wonder if Nana's eyesight was failing and she'd accidentally bought me some kind of grim "Condolences for the death of your beloved parakeet" card.

When I pulled it open, a silver chain slithered out and landed with a succession of delicate clinks in a coil on the kitchen counter.

That's odd, I thought. *If she wanted to give me a necklace, why wouldn't she wrap it or put it in a box or something?*

When I picked up the chain and held it under the sunlight beaming in through the large window above the sink, it seemed to take on a strange glow, as though its links were covered in tiny diamonds that picked up every subtlety of the sun's rays.

Puzzled, I set the chain down on the counter while I scanned the inside of the card.

Instead of her usual "For a very lovely girl on her birthday," Nana had written an enigmatic note in her tidy script.

Happy Seventeenth Birthday, Vega.

Today marks a turning point: the end of an old life and the beginning of a new one. There are challenges and danger ahead. Wear this silver chain at all times. It will never tangle or break. Perhaps it will save your life as it once saved mine.

Love,
Nana.

My mother had always referred to my grandmother as an "eccentric character." Will and I had always half-jokingly speculated that she was some sort of sorceress who made potions out of eye of newt, tail of squirrel, or liver of the neighbor's pet goldfish. Her cottage in Cornwall was a veritable museum of strange and wonderful artifacts, ranging from unidentifiable animal skulls to medieval-looking weaponry to vials of substances I'd always imagined were magical balms and tonics, but which my mother had pointed out were probably just standard kitchen sauces and seasonings.

Still, sending me a "life-saving" silver chain was a little out there, even for Nana.

"Well," I muttered, tucking the card back into the envelope and fastening the chain around my neck by its delicate clasp, "Today I learned that my grandmother has gone completely batcrap crazy. Happy Birthday to me."

THE BOY AND THE BOOK

I HAD JUST PICKED UP THE ARMY SURPLUS SATCHEL THAT SERVED AS my purse when the doorbell rang. The second I yanked the front door open, Liv pounced, squeezing me so hard I was sure I'd pass out from the loss of circulation.

"Hello, Birthday Girl!" she shouted when she'd pulled away, strands of jet-black hair bouncing as she hopped up and down. "Let's go! I want to hit Perks for a mochaccino after my little surprise. All my parents had at the cottage was instant coffee that tasted like dirty puddle water funneled through an old sweat sock."

"Feeding a caffeine addiction when you're already a hyperactive lunatic seems like a really bad idea, Liv. Maybe you should see if they sell chamomile tea. Or better still, horse tranquilizers. A mochaccino might send you flying over the edge into Loopy-Town."

"Pfft! Loopy-Town is underrated. Come on," she said, grabbing my sleeve and pulling like a puppy desperate to play. "Let's head out. It's a perfect day."

I followed her outside, locking the door behind me before

tucking my key into my bag and jogging toward the sidewalk to keep up with her quick pace.

The street was lined with mature trees whose limbs drooped over the road, forming a large archway that Will and I had always described as our own private tunnel when we were kids. In our imaginations we'd turned Fairhaven into a veritable amusement park filled with interesting nooks and crannies. We knew which trees were best for climbing, which parts of the woods were best for finding berries, and which back yards had the best treehouses.

Much as I was looking forward to one day leaving this town, I did love the comfort of its familiar streets and neighborhoods. The old houses with stories to tell, the wrap-around porches where people sat quietly in the summer months, watching the world pass them by. I loved that I knew the name of every dog on our block, and that they often came out to greet me as I passed by.

I'd lost so much in this town when my parents had died that part of me wanted to leave and never look back. But Fairhaven held so many warm memories that it was hard to imagine ever fully letting it go. Still, with Will leaving for college, there was little to keep me here.

"So," I said, hoping to take my mind off the pending assault of loneliness, "I feel like I should ask you what terrible birthday surprise you're about to throw my way, Liv."

She shot me a shifty sideways glance before she began to skip along the sidewalk like an excited five-year-old who really needs to pee. "Okay, I'll tell you," she said. "Two words: Callum. Drake. You're going to love him so much. He's tall and handsome, and he has the nicest—"

"Wait. Whoa. Stop for a sec! What are you even talking about?"

"Callum Drake!" Liv repeated, like that should have cleared everything up. "He's just started working at the Novel Hovel."

The Hovel had been my favorite place in the world since the moment I'd learned to read. I'd stopped in at least once a month for the last ten years, whether I intended to buy anything or not. I don't know if it was the smell of the place, the reverential silence, or the opportunity it gave me to take a break from the world, but I considered the smallish bookshop my safe haven and my home away from home.

It was not, however, a place I associated with checking out boys.

"Are you serious?" I asked, my brows meeting in something approaching anger.

"Just wait until you see him..." Liv's voice trailed off like she was about to swoon into a Victorian, mid-sentence faint. "He's easily the hottest guy Fairhaven has ever seen. He's tall—did I already say that? So tall."

"Uh-huh."

"He's also *sooo* smart. He knows everything about everything. Not to mention he has the most incredible cheekbones and the best accent. Oh man, his accent..."

"What accent?" I asked.

"He's English. At least I think he is."

"So what? My grandmother is English."

"Yeah, well, Callum isn't your grandmother, believe me. His voice is like velvet and silk got together and took a bath in melted chocolate."

"Sounds delicious. And completely undigestible. How do you even know about this guy? You've been gone for ages."

"My parents had him over for dinner after we got home yesterday. I mean, they had him and his *parents* over. His father just started working in my dad's law office. So basically, I got to stare across our dining room table at Callum for two whole hours last night, which was amazing." In typical fashion, she was rambling a mile a minute, the words coming faster than an auctioneer's. "He even eats chicken parmigiana like a Roman god. The point is, you're going to lose your mind over him."

"Uh-huh. Tell me, when have I ever lost my mind over a guy?"

"Never. Because you're infuriatingly chaste, not to mention downright hostile toward every guy you meet," Liv laughed. "You have to promise me you'll be nice to him, though. He's so...dreamy."

"Dreamy? Really? Did we just time-warp back to the 1950s? Does he have his hair slicked back and a pack of cigarettes rolled up in the sleeve of his white t-shirt?"

Liv gave me a dismissive wave of her hand. "I promise, you'll die twice before you hit the ground when you lay eyes on him."

"In that case, I hope I never lay my eyes on him. I know it's weird, but I generally prefer being alive."

"Well, the point is, you have to meet him, if for no other reason than that he was asking about you."

"Oh? Why's that?" I asked, doing my best to pretend I didn't much care about the answer.

Liv shrugged. "Dunno. He just said he'd heard there was a girl called Vega who liked to come into the shop. It seems your book-wormishness has made you famous. But it sounds like you're not interested in him, so we'll just have to see how you feel when you actually meet him."

"Works for me."

Liv let the subject drop, and we walked in silence for a time, enjoying the fresh air and cool breeze.

"Oh, hey," she finally blurted out, "are you going to Midsummer Fest tonight?"

I'd all but forgotten about the candlelit procession and rowdy parade that took place downtown each year on the last Friday of July. Nearly everyone in town showed up at sundown, dressed in masks of all kinds, from cutesy animal heads to terrifying monsters. The strange, noisy gathering made its way down a series of residential streets, candles and noise-makers in hand, before finishing at the entrance to Norfolk Commons, the town's one and only large park. No one seemed to know how the tradition had started, but the whole thing amounted to a creepy, feral parade I sort of enjoyed. Much as I usually abhorred socializing, the anonymity provided by a mask made this particular public outing almost tolerable.

"I'm not sure I'm going," I replied. "I mean, maybe I will, I don't know. It depends."

"What the hell kind of wishy-washy answer is that?" Liv laughed, shouldering me so hard I went stumbling off the sidewalk onto someone's front lawn.

"You know me," I said, skipping back onto the concrete walkway. "*Non-committal* is my middle name. Anyhow, Will's getting home today, so I'll go if he—"

"What?" Liv squealed, her eyes going wide as she stopped in her tracks and turned my way. "Will's going to be in town? When can I see him? How long will he be here? You *have* to tell him to come out tonight. I need to see my future husband just once before he goes off to college."

I barely suppressed the desire to fake-gag. Liv's unabashed, ongoing crush on my older brother had begun when she was about seven years old, and she'd never made any effort whatsoever to hide it, despite the fact that Will had consistently treated her like nothing more than his little sister's best friend.

"I'm sure he'd regret it if he missed out on an opportunity to get drooled on by his insane future wife before he takes off for four years."

Liv snort-laughed. "If you two *do* show up at Midsummer Fest, keep an eye out for me. I'll be wearing a giant zebra head."

"Of course you will," I replied, inhaling a deep breath of fresh air as we approached Norfolk Commons, the sprawling park where the Midsummer Fest Procession would be held that evening. As Liv and I turned onto High Street and began to pass the park, we saw the endless strings of lights draped on all the trees in preparation for the evening's festivities.

Two security officers in yellow reflective vests were cordoning off an area by one of the concessions stands where the ladies from St. Francis Church would be selling an array of cookies and confections later that night. Just beyond them, a crew of groundskeepers was busy trimming some of the hedges, cutting the grass, and hauling large brown sacks of branches and leaves over to a big blue pickup truck parked halfway across the jogging path.

As Liv and I passed, one of the groundskeepers, a tall man I'd never seen before, looked at me and narrowed his dark eyes, lifting a hand as though he was about to wave but thought better of it. I peered over at Liv to see if she'd noticed, but she was busy yammering on about how much she was looking forward to wearing her zebra's head that night. When I turned to look back, the stranger was still staring at me, sending a chill skittering down my spine.

"Did you see that?" I asked Liv.

"See what?"

"That man—the one in the coveralls. He just looked at me and kind of waved, like he knew me."

"Does he?" she asked, turning around to look.

"I don't think so. I'm pretty sure I'd remember that face."

"Maybe he sensed it was your special day and was sending you mental happy birthday wishes."

"Yeah," I said with a guffaw. "I'm sure that's it."

"Come on," Liv replied with a shrug. "Let's cross here."

Grabbing me by the hand, she practically dragged me across the street and over to the Novel Hovel. The clunky brass bell hanging above the door to the bookstore clanged to announce our arrival, and we stepped into the musty shop, Liv in full golden retriever mode as she scanned the place for her mysterious dreamboat.

"Down, girl," I commanded, wishing I had a leash.

"You should be hunting for him, too," Liv insisted. "You don't get what you want without going after it."

"What I want right now is to find something to read other than what Mrs. Romanowski is going to assign us in English class this year."

Liv paused and gave me a long, accusing look. "You already read all the books on her syllabus, didn't you?"

"Maybe."

"Nerd."

"Zebra head."

"And proud of it. Anyhow, I'm going to look for Mr. Handsome-Face, since you're being a lame-ass."

"Enjoy your prowling," I replied with a wink. "I'll be on the hunt for a few good books to hook up with."

As Liv ducked down the Philosophy and Self-Help aisle, I split off and made my way to the sale table at the back of the store where I picked up the closest book I could find, a collection of essays about the history of women in war, and began to leaf through it.

"That's an excellent choice," said a deep, English-accented voice from just behind me. "The essay by Margaret Billingsly on Florence Nightingale is especially perceptive. I highly recommend it."

I knew before I'd even turned around that this had to be the boy Liv described. The voice. The knowledge. The accent, which was nothing at all like my grandmother's, yet oddly similar. It was lilting, like waves washing up on a pebble-coated beach. It was the kind of voice that made everything seem right with the world...the kind of voice that could become addictive very quickly.

Which meant that I needed to counter it with a smart-ass remark as soon as humanly possible.

But when I swung around to reply, I found myself gasping instead.

Liv had been dead wrong about Callum Drake's looks.

He wasn't merely handsome.

He was exquisitely beautiful—in a polished, broad-shouldered, diamond-blue-eyed kind of way that made me wish a hole would open up in the floor and swallow me whole so I could escape his blinding perfection.

He was at least six-foot-two, with a strong, square jaw, and he carried himself with a confidence no seventeen-year-old should have. To make matters worse, he was wearing a form-fitting blood red t-shirt and dark jeans that showed off the powerful build of an athlete.

Damn you, Liv, for bringing me here.

Despite the casualness of the boy's attire, something in his face and demeanor was oddly elegant. Regal, even. But the most disconcerting thing of all was the way he was looking at me, like he could see right through me. I couldn't seem to fight off the feeling that he was reading my thoughts and emotions all at once, without even trying.

My heart started hammering in my chest, perspiration pooling at the small of my back, and I found myself wishing for a distraction—another customer, a fire alarm, an alien invasion—anything I might use as a legitimate excuse to look away.

Suddenly I remembered I was holding a book. I set it down and shrugged, hoping Callum didn't see my jaw clench up with nervous excitement. "It's not my usual fare," I said as coolly as possible. "I prefer slow, plodding novels with zero plot, terrible characters, and nothing perceptive about them at all."

"A masochist, then?"

I was just getting ready to stammer out a response when Liv came shrieking around a corner.

"Callum, there you are! This is Vega Sloane!" she said, skidding up and stopping just shy of barreling into the guy's chest.

"You were asking about her last night. She's my bestie. Her father's side of the family is from England, just like you!" She offered up the information as if it should be enough to cement our engagement and subsequent happy marriage.

"Vega. Like the star in the Lyra constellation," Callum said. "It suits you." Smiling, he held out a hand.

I was frozen, my mind twisting around itself as I tried to figure out what I was supposed to do. Did I shake his hand? Did anyone *ever* shake the hand of a boy who was as beautiful as he was? There was something so noble, so otherworldly about this boy-who-looked-like-a-man who was busy looking into my eyes, reading my soul like he was flipping through the morning paper. He looked like he should be leading an army or ruling a country from a golden throne, not standing here talking to someone like me in the middle of a dusty old bookstore.

Idiot, I told myself. *He's not a demi-god. He's just some teenager with a Wikipedia-like intellect, impossibly perfect features, an amazing voice, and...a mesmerizing smile.*

Damn him.

Grumbling internally at myself, I pressed my hand into his and shook it, trying my hardest to relax my tense body. "Hi," I murmured.

"Hi." He looked amused, like my embarrassing awkwardness was entertaining him. I couldn't help wondering if every girl he met reacted the same way.

"And yes, it's like the star," I said. "My name, I mean." I chewed nervously on the inside of my cheek, but I still didn't pull my gaze away for fear that if I did so, he might disappear.

Liv let out a third-grade giggle. "Jeez, Vega, if you're going to stare like that, why don't you just snap a photo with your phone?" she asked.

I shot her a glare, my cheeks heating with mortification. "Sorry," I said, pulling my eyes to the floor. "I just…"

"You're just confused about which book you want to read,"

Callum said, reaching past me to the table and grabbing a thick white paperback with a sword on its cover. Either he was oblivious to the fact I'd been gawking at him, or he was kind enough to *pretend* to be oblivious. Either way, I was grateful. "Might I suggest this one?" he asked. "It'll take you out of this world and put you in a whole new one. Which, in my experience, is never a bad thing."

"Have you read it?" I asked, glancing at the cover without registering any information whatsoever.

"I have. Something tells me you'll find it very…informative."

"Okay," I replied, mesmerized by his unbelievable eyes, which seemed to shimmer in the dull light of the dusty shop. It must have been the energy-saving overhead bulbs that did it. No one's eyes naturally looked like limpid pools I suddenly and inexplicably wanted to go skinny dipping in.

Yeah, that was it. Definitely the light bulbs.

"I'll give it a shot," I said.

"Oh, hey! It's Vega's birthday!" Liv interrupted, clearly bored by all the book talk.

"Is that so?" Callum asked as he led us to the front of the shop and slipped around behind the counter. "In that case, I definitely can't let you pay for the book." He reached down and pulled a paper bag from underneath the counter. He slipped the novel inside the bag and he held it out to me, a glint of amusement in those perfect blue eyes.

"Oh, I couldn't…" I began, but he shook his head.

"Of course you can. Happy Birthday, Vega."

I smiled. The way he said my name was oddly soothing, like he'd added music to the two syllables. His voice really was unlike any I'd ever heard. Maybe it was his particular accent, or else an odd hint of maturity most teenage boys lacked. I was so used to hearing squeaky-voiced adolescents who hadn't quite grown into manhood. Either way, it was a nice change from the usual.

As I took the package from Callum, his fingers grazed against mine, sending a shock of heat to my cheeks. I told myself I shouldn't enjoy the accidental contact nearly so much. There was a danger in the fleeting moment of pleasure, the sort of emotional risk I'd shielded myself from for years, and the thought of becoming vulnerable now both thrilled and terrified me.

"Any special plans for your birthday? Are you going out tonight?" he asked, which only accelerated my raging pulse once again. Boys didn't usually ask me what I was up to on a Friday night. Then again, boys didn't usually speak to me at all.

Liv elbowed me impatiently as if to say *Stop being a mute idiot.*

"I…I might go to Midsummer Fest tonight," I shrugged. "I'm not really into birthdays, ever since my parents…I mean, I'm just not into birthdays."

"Me neither," he replied, an odd flash of sympathy slipping over his face. "Once you've had enough of them, they all begin to blend into one another."

I narrowed my eyes at him. He couldn't have been much older than I was, yet he was talking as if he'd had eighty birthdays and had grown sick of them.

"Are you going to be there, Callum?" Liv asked. "At Midsummer Fest, I mean."

"I will," he replied. "I figure it's a great way to get to know the town."

"More like a way to find out how weird our town is," I said.

"True," Callum replied. "Of course, one person's weird is another person's wonderful."

"And which are you?" I asked, stunned that such a brazen comment came out of my usually reserved mouth.

"I believe," he said with a wry smile, "that's for you to find out."

After a moment of strained silence, I finally blurted out, "Well, we should get going. Liv needs her caffeine. It seems she hasn't bounced off enough walls today."

"Fair enough. Enjoy, Liv." Callum said before softly adding, "Take care, Vega. Watch for strangers." From the tone of his voice, he sounded as though he was genuinely concerned that something might happen to me. Which was odd…but sort of sweet, too.

"I will," I replied, daring another look at him as I drew in a deep breath, trying in vain to calm my out-of-control heart.

"Hey, I just got a really good idea!" Liv said to Callum. "Do you want to come to Perks with us?"

I gasped, terrified and excited at the prospect of spending more time in his presence.

The boy with the impossibly blue eyes pulled his gaze away from me, shaking his head. "I can't, unfortunately," he said. "I'm in charge of looking after the shop today."

"Too bad," Liv replied, grabbing me by the arm and yanking me toward the door. "Well, I suppose we'll see you tonight, then?"

"Tonight," he replied. "I'm looking forward to it."

I gave him a feeble wave goodbye, which he returned with a raised hand and a mysterious, slightly ominous smile.

COFFEE TALK

When we stepped outside, Liv let out a squeal, grabbed my arm, and squeezed hard.

"Ow!" I said. "What was that for?"

"Did you *see* how he was staring at you?"

"I don't know what you're talking about."

She let go and crossed her arms in an irritated pout. "Are you kidding me right now? Callum didn't take his eyes off you the whole time we were in there."

"I hadn't noticed," I shrugged.

"Well, that's total B.S. Anyone sane would feel those eyes on her, even if you weren't looking—which you totally were, by the way. Come on, Vega. He's so into you. You should ask him out."

"Or—and hear me out on this—I could *not* ask him out."

Liv rolled her eyes so hard I was sure she spotted her brain. "You're so frustrating!" she yelled as a couple of joggers dodged their way around us. "You two have so much in common."

"Okay, I'll bite. What exactly do we have in common? We're both bi-pedal carbon-based forms of life?"

"He likes books. You like books."

"Half the universe likes books."

"He looks like a Greek god sculpted out of marble, and you're super-pretty, in spite of the fact that you insist on wearing those awful hoodies and hiding your amazing hair all the time."

Shrugging off her backwards compliments, I said, "I have nothing to talk to him about."

"You could tell him about your trips to England."

"I hardly think he wants to hear about some stupid American high school student hopping across the pond and being a tourist in his native land."

"Fine." Liv threw her arms up, clearly exasperated. "Then just make out with him and then tell me if he's a good kisser."

"Ugh. Tell me, do your hormones have an off-switch?"

"Not that I've found."

I turned and began walking toward the coffee shop down the street. "And now we come to the *actual* point," I laughed.

"Come on!" Liv whined. "I don't have a boyfriend. I probably never will, unless your brother finally asks me out. Until then I need to live vicariously through you."

"Then you'll have to live vicariously through a boring single person, because no way am I asking that guy out. If you're so hot for him, why don't you make a move?"

"Because he's perfect for you! What kind of wingman would I be if I snatched up your Mr. Right?"

"Wing*woman*."

"What?"

"You'd be my wingwoman, not my wing*man*."

"Either way, I promise to be by your side and protecting your flank when you spread your wings and swoop in for the kill."

"I'm not sure what's more Liv-esque. Your tireless persistence or your unbelievably mixed metaphors."

"We can figure that out when I go to make my Maid of Honor toast at your wedding."

"Slow down, Wingwoman. I have a strict rule about not marrying anybody on my seventeenth birthday."

Liv let out a hearty laugh accompanied by an equally powerful hug right in the middle of the sidewalk, which ended with me laughing along with her until we were both teary-eyed and choking for air.

I might have considered her attempted set-up if not for the fact that Callum was intimidatingly handsome. I could barely look him in the eye. But it wasn't just that. There was something else—the disconcerting feeling that he could see right through me. I wasn't sure if it was his confidence or the way he carried himself. Or the weird feeling I got that he had somehow packed a century's worth of living into his seventeen years.

As we made our way toward the end of the block, Liv leaned in close and whispered, "Great. Charlie's out front of Perks." She gestured toward the homeless man in a tattered grey coat who was sitting on the sidewalk out front of the café, a large German Shepherd by his side. "I suppose you'll want to say 'Hi' to him."

I nodded. "Sure. Why not? I don't base my civility on how much money someone has in their bank account."

"I never understand why he stays in Fairhaven," she said. "No one except for you ever gives him money. He'd make a lot more in a big city." The moment she'd spoken, she shot me a remorseful sideways glance and added, "Not that I mind him being here."

"Maybe he likes this town because it's pretty," I replied. "Who knows? He must do okay. It's not like he and Rufus are starving."

"That's because you're always giving them food, Saint Vega."

She was right. I'd always made a point of greeting Charlie and Rufus as I passed by, and on days when I could, I'd always given them a little something to eat or drink. I supposed I felt like I could relate to both of them. Like me, they didn't entirely fit into society, at least not on society's terms. They were outcasts who lived on the periphery, watching the world pass them by as if they were invisible. It was a position I sympathized with all too well.

As we approached, I could hear Charlie humming some unidentifiable tune. His voice was low and gravelly, and the sound wasn't exactly pretty, but for some reason it still made me smile.

"Hey, Charlie," I said as Liv and I stepped up to front doors of the café. "Want a coffee?"

"You've gotta buy it," he said curtly, turning one of his empty pants pockets inside out. "I got no money."

"Fair enough. I'll buy this time," I said with a wink. "But the next one's on you."

He smiled his broken, yellow-toothed smile and said, "Deal."

I considered mentioning it was my birthday and I'd do it as a gift to myself, but I didn't want to attract any extra attention. The truth was, though I was way too embarrassed to ever admit it to Liv, I was still trembling from my encounter with Callum. "Wait here."

"Where else do ya think I'd go?" Charlie asked with a shrug.

When I ducked into the coffee shop, I ordered a large with cream and sugar and a chocolate donut, while Liv asked for some sort of fancy, frothy, whipped cream, cinnamon mocha concoction that was sounded more complicated than any equation I'd learned in algebra class. As I sidled up next to her, a long line of customers began to gather behind us.

"Must be the late-morning crowd," I said as I grabbed my order. "I'm going to bring this to Charlie. I'll meet you outside."

"You don't want something?" Liv asked. "I'll buy! It's the least I can do, considering I didn't get you a real gift, other than the hottie in the bookstore."

"I'm good," I said. "But thanks."

When I'd squeezed through the growing group of customers and out the front door, I handed the coffee and donut to Charlie, who took them with a nod and a grunt, before turning away as if to let me know he was in no mood for further conversation. I stepped away, giving him space, only to see Liv skip back outside, an enormous whipped-cream-topped beverage in hand.

"What do you want to do now?" she asked with a grin. "We could hang out in the park. You can check out your new book while I watch the cute boys passing by."

"Actually, that sounds like an excellent plan."

Without a second's hesitation, we turned to head over to the nearby crosswalk.

But we'd only gone about five feet down the sidewalk when a deep, echoing voice from behind us stopped me in my tracks.

"Vega Sloane," the eerie voice rumbled. *"I have a gift for you."*

THE GIFT

THE WAY THE WORDS VIBRATED THROUGH THE AIR SENT A SHIVER down my spine.

The voice wasn't Charlie's. It couldn't be.

And yet it *had* to be. I could feel in the marrow of my bones that the words had somehow emerged from his mouth.

I turned to Liv, who was standing frozen next to me, her eyes focused on something in the distance. She looked as though she was too freaked out to move, and I couldn't say I blamed her. I twisted around to see Charlie standing in the middle of the sidewalk, his eyes locked on mine. Rufus was alert at his side, his ears pricked up, tail tucked between his legs. But something was…off.

"What the…?" I gasped. "What happened to you?"

Charlie's normally dull, dark brown eyes had turned gold, his irises flickering as bright as the scales on a goldfish. Rufus' eyes, too, had changed to a fiery shade of yellowish-orange.

I slammed my eyes shut, trying to will away the impossibility of it all. But when I opened them again, the man and his dog were still standing in front of me, glowing eyes still firmly locked on my own. I glanced around, hoping to see pedestrians stopping and staring at the two odd creatures. I needed someone to confirm that I wasn't losing my mind.

But aside from my best friend, the street was eerily empty.

I reached out for Liv, whose eyes were still fixed, unblinking, on something in the distance.

"Hey," I whispered, squeezing her forearm. "Turn around. You need to see this."

But she didn't react. Didn't move. Didn't seem to hear me at all. I poked her with my finger, but her shoulder felt hard and unyielding. She didn't so much as flinch, let alone answer me.

It was then I realized the rest of the world had come to a stop, too. The cars on the street had gone stone still. The leaves of the fluttering, summer trees had frozen in mid-rustle.

Not a single bird was flying through the air or chirping in the treetops. The crisp breeze that had been whistling around all morning had gone eerily mute. No one was walking along the sidewalk, and none of the usual cars was cruising by, despite the fact we were standing on Fairhaven's busiest street at one of its busiest times of day.

"What's going on?" I asked, turning back to face Charlie, who was still staring at me, his chest heaving with effort.

"I have something for you," he said, his breathing choked off and labored like he was trying to talk underwater. "On your seventeenth birthday."

"Forget my birthday," I nearly shouted, making a sweeping gesture at the frozen-in-time scene around us. "Everything just stopped!"

"We haven't," he gurgled. "As for you, you're just getting ready to start."

"Wait—how did you even know it's my birthday?"

Instead of replying, he raised his left arm and held something out in his palm. A small red box, no bigger than a deck of playing cards. A silver ribbon was tied neatly around it, shining bright in the sunlight.

I looked down at Rufus, searching his face for a sign. His tail flicked back and forth in what seemed like some kind of canine encouragement, his tongue dangling out in a friendly pant. His eyes were still a few fiery shades of gold, but otherwise he was behaving like a relatively normal dog.

"Okay, buddy," I said. "But I'm holding you responsible if something horrible happens to me."

Rufus let out a loud bark.

I inched forward and took the elegant little package from Charlie's outstretched hand. "What is this?"

But when I pulled my eyes up to Charlie's again, the odd glow had left his irises. He was shaking his head, like he couldn't figure out where he was or what was happening.

"What?" he growled in his usual low rumble. "What'd you say?"

"I was asking…what…this…"

As I spoke, the world started up again, as if someone had turned an ignition key and coaxed it to life. To my right, a car whizzed by. Behind Charlie, the café's door opened, and a woman came striding out, excusing herself impatiently while he backed out of her way, pulling Rufus with him. I looked down to see that the dog's eyes had also reverted to their usual dark brown. Now ignoring me, the pair plopped themselves back down in their usual spot, with Charlie muttering something unintelligible as he picked up the coffee I'd bought him and took a long swig.

"Vega!" Liv called out from up ahead on the sidewalk. "What's the hold-up?"

"Sorry," I said, forcing the tremor out of my voice. "I…thought I dropped something back here."

Shoving the red box into my bag, I turned her way. "You didn't happen to notice anything weird just now, did you?"

"Besides you pretending not to be into Callum and then

buying a coffee and a donut for a guy you hardly know and his dog? No. Nothing weird about any of that at all."

Just as Liv shot me a skeptical look, a *Bleep-Bloop!* sound erupted from inside her jacket pocket. "Oh, crapola!" she said, pulling her phone out and reading the message on its screen. "I forgot I have a dentist's appointment at eleven. My mom's wondering where I am." She stared at the screen for a second before looking up again. "I'm going to have to take a rain check on the park. I'm so sorry!"

"It's fine," I replied with a withering smile. "Totally fine." *I mean, I'm pretty sure I've lost my mind, but other than that, no worries.*

She pulled me in for a quick, one-armed birthday hug. "Have a great day. I'll see you tonight!" she said before dashing in the direction of home, her icy mocha monstrosity still in hand.

Reaching into my satchel to make sure I hadn't imagined Charlie's gift, I jogged across the street to Norfolk Commons and slipped through the large wrought iron gate. I headed for the first unoccupied park bench I saw, all the while trying to calm my racing heart. Drawing my hood up over my head, I plopped down, pulled the package out of my bag, and set it down in my lap.

"Should I open you?" I asked, perfectly aware of how idiotic it was to ask an inanimate object such a question. Or any question, for that matter. After staring at it for several seconds to reassure myself it wasn't going to explode, I picked it up, held it to my ear, and shook it.

I couldn't hear anything.

Holding my breath, I tugged at the end of the silver bow holding the box shut, and the glittering fabric slipped loose in my hand. I put my fingers on the box's lid and lifted it open, wincing as I did. Charlie was a nice guy and all, but a sudden thought flashed through my mind that the gift could easily be a dead mouse or something equally repulsive Rufus had found behind a dumpster.

I swear, Charlie. If this is gift-wrapped doggie poop, I'm going to dump the next cup of coffee I buy for you on your head.

Inside the box, though, was a delicate golden cloth, wrapped around an object. The cloth itself was exquisitely beautiful, as though it was spun from the finest gold thread.

"Wow," I gasped, stunned at its opulence.

I picked up a corner of the delicate fabric between my fingers and lifted it, peering underneath. It was then that the strangest item met my eyes: a silver key so ornate that at first, I didn't recognize what it was.

Its head was shaped like a vicious, fire-breathing dragon. Just below that was a dark red gem, surrounded by what appeared to be a frame of small diamonds.

I stared in wonder at the trinket. I'd never seen anything like it. The piece was intriguing, like something a medieval magician might have worn on a long chain around his neck while concocting spells or zapping lightning bolts at the king's enemies or whatever it was those guys used to do.

Picking up the key, for the first time I felt its substantial weight in my hands. For some reason, it seemed heavier than the package had. I slid a finger over the gems, trying to determine if they were real. "No, of course they're not," I chuckled to myself. "A homeless guy wouldn't be likely to go handing teenagers precious gems. If they were real, the key would have to be worth thousands of dollars…and I don't think Charlie's exactly wealthy."

So where had it come from, exactly? Was it some carnival prize? A novelty paperweight from the office supply store over on Victoria?

For a moment I contemplated going back to ask Charlie who'd put him up to this stunt. Was it something my brother Will had set up? It had to be some sort of elaborate hoax. But why would he give me a key, especially one like this? Maybe it was a skeleton key, the sort that would open an ancient treasure chest or some forbidden room in a gothic mansion.

As I was trying to figure out what to do, I noticed a piece of paper tucked inside the box, under the bottom fold of the gold cloth. My fingers shaking, I reached in and drew it out.

The handwriting was elegant, the words written in a scrolling calligraphy. I had no idea who could possibly have managed to write so tidily on such a small scrap of paper. Then again, that seemed like the least of today's mysteries.

The words on the paper were even more bizarre than the penmanship:

Vega,

This key will open many doors. Some friendly, some deadly.

You are a Seeker.

Prove yourself worthy, and you may just save the world.

THE WOMAN

For what felt like several minutes of profound confusion, my eyes moved back and forth between the ornate key and the note as my brain tried in vain to process the dream-like weirdness of everything that had happened since I'd woken up this morning. The odd gift and message from my Nana. Charlie and Rufus's glowing eyes. The frozen moment in time. The key. And now the note, which, oddly enough, was the most puzzling element of them all.

"I'm being filmed," I muttered, looking around at the assorted people and passersby in the park. "I know I'm being filmed."

To test out my theory, I jumped up and waved my hand in the air at what I was sure must be a park full of cleverly hidden cameras. But other than startling a passing jogger who hopped to the side and gave me the stink-eye as he passed, I got no reaction.

Still on the lookout for the host of a reality show to come bursting out of the bushes, I tucked the key into the pocket of my hoodie and zipped it up. I began to walk in the direction of home, my eyes still fixed on the note in my right hand.

I'd gone about twenty feet when I nearly collided with someone.

"Watch where you're going!" a shrill feminine voice snarled.

I pulled my eyes up to see a tall, elegant woman with bobbed, white-blond hair staring down at me. Her blue eyes were icy, the color of the sky on a cold winter's day, and as she glared, her thin, shapely eyebrows met in a fierce expression of disgust. A coat of dark red lipstick accentuated the angry sneer on her lips.

"Sorry," I muttered, folding up the note and jamming it into my bag.

"What's that you have there?" she asked, eyeing the satchel strapped over my shoulder.

"What?"

"In your bag."

"Why? Are you mugging me or something?"

The woman pulled her eyes to mine once again. Now, they no longer looked entirely blue. Instead, they seemed to have begun dancing with other colors: Gold. Red. Silver. I stared at them, mesmerized for a moment. Was it a trick of the light? Shadows dancing over her face from the tree limbs above us?

"Of course I wasn't going to mug you," she said, her voice taking on a smooth, charming edge as her eyes settled into a deep blue once again. "I'm so pleased to have found you, daughter of Viviane."

"Um, yeah, I think you've got the wrong person," I stammered. "My mother's name is...Sarah." I deliberately avoided telling her I had no mother. I could just see the psycho following me home once she figured out I was living on my own.

Shooting her as menacing a sneer as I could manage, I started to walk again, my knees trembling as I waited for her to pounce on me from behind. I'd had enough of freaky eyes and weird talk for one morning. All I wanted was to get home, shut the door, and spend the rest of my birthday quietly pretending none of this happened. But before I'd taken three steps, the woman reached out and grabbed my forearm, gripping hard enough to make me wince.

I twisted around to confront her, my jaw tensing with a sudden shot of fear.

Someone help me, I thought desperately. *Anyone, please. I need help.*

It was a strange impulse for me to ask for rescue, even tacitly. I'd grown so used to fending for myself and looking after my own needs that the very idea of leaning on anyone else was foreign to me. But right now, all I wanted was for someone to swoop in and save me from this menacing weirdo.

"Let go of me!" I shouted. I tried to rip my arm away, but the woman was oddly strong, her knuckles white as her grip tightened.

"I can't do that," she said, shaking her head, a disconcerting smile on her lips. "You're the one we came to find. They say you're the one who will—"

She stopped talking, slamming her mouth shut.

"Get off of me!" I hissed, my fear turning quickly to rage.

The woman, who had apparently lost her train of thought, released my arm and backed away, her eyes brimming with terror. For a second, I felt triumphant, like I'd scared her into submission with my commanding voice and expression of pure ire.

It only took a moment to realize that it wasn't me who'd caused her to freeze, but something behind me.

Horrified that a new threat was approaching, I spun around to see a fuzzy blur sprinting in our direction at lightning speed.

Before I could process what was happening, Rufus had leapt up and thrown all his weight at the terrified woman, slamming her backwards onto the ground. I backed away, my eyes locked on the dog, who was alternating between growling at her and staring up at me, tongue out, as though he was looking for approval. His eyes had gone gold again, an inexplicable light shining from inside him.

As I stared at him, a voice rumbled its way through my mind.

I had no idea where it was coming from, but the words felt like they were spoken by someone so close I could feel them vibrating through my bones. Low and deep, the voice didn't sound quite human…although I couldn't say what it *did* sound like.

I opened my mouth to ask Rufus if he was the one speaking to me. But no, of course he wasn't. That would have been completely off the rails.

"Get away, Vega," the voice said. *"Get far away from the woman right now. Don't offer it to her, whatever you do. Protect it with your life."*

"Protect what? What's going on?" I asked the air, my head twisting around to identify the speaker's location.

The woman on the ground tried to say something, but Rufus shoved his muzzle in her face and let out a low growl, forcing her to slam her mouth shut.

"Go, Vega!" the voice repeated, this time more urgently. *"Before she gets her hands on you again."*

The voice might have been mysteriously disembodied, but the advice was solid. I turned and sprinted away as fast as my legs would carry me. I darted through the park's gate only to be stopped in my tracks when a tall figure stepped directly into my path.

I let out a shriek only to realize that Callum Drake was standing in front of me. Without a word he reached for my shoulders, the heat from his palms sinking deep into my skin as I struggled to calm my harrowed breaths. Staring into my eyes with the same look I'd seen in the bookshop—the one that made me feel like he could read me—he loosened his grip but still held me steady, a much-needed support for which I was grateful. I felt like I was about to pass out, and he was the only thing keeping me from sinking to the ground.

"Vega," he said, "Are you all right?"

I shook my head. Maybe it was the tears welling up in my eyes that made his irises look as though they were glowing in the sunlight, a shade of blue seeming to radiate both hot and cold at once. A sudden urge possessed me to bury myself against his chest and ask him to hold me. But instead, I wrapped my arms around myself and trembled.

"What happened?" he asked.

"There was a woman," I said. "She..." I spun around, looking for the well-dressed lunatic who'd been lying on the ground and the dog who'd pinned her, but all I saw was a scruffy gray squirrel hopping across the path about twenty feet away.

"I don't understand," I said under my breath.

"Something's freaked you out," Callum said. "Come on, I'll take you home."

I shook my head again. "You have to work. It's okay, I can get there on my own."

"I'm sure you can. Let me at least get you inside the shop to catch your breath. You look like you've seen a ghost eating another ghost. Don't worry," he added as I started to protest, "I'm on my lunch break."

I nodded, too shaken to resist.

He put a protective arm around my shoulder and guided me across the street toward the bookstore, which had a quickly-scrawled "Back in Five Minutes" note taped inside the front door. When we arrived, he led me inside, locking the door behind us.

"Callum," I said, "You're sure I'm okay to stay here a minute?" My eyes were moving between him and the window. I was fully expecting someone—or maybe something—to come crashing into the place. "I don't want to get you in any trouble."

"Mr. Worrell won't care. From what I hear, you're his best customer."

"I don't mean about that," I said, glancing out the window to the street where strange events seemed to be tagging along after me like a litter of insane and potentially dangerous puppies.

"You can stay here as long as you like," he said, stepping closer. He reached up and pushed a strand of hair behind my ear.

The heat in his touch was a comfort, a reminder that he and I were both alive and safe. "What happened out there?"

"The woman I mentioned," I said. "She was really weird. I mean, she looked wealthy and elegant, but she was so...creepy. She grabbed me, but Rufus stopped her..."

"Rufus?" Callum asked.

"Charlie's dog..." I shook my head. "You know what? It doesn't matter. This has been the craziest morning of my life, and to be honest I'm not sure I really want to talk about it."

"Of course." We stared at one another for a moment before Callum puffed out a quick breath.

"Listen," he said, "I should really help get you home. Where do you live? I can offer you a ride."

"It's not far. I can walk."

"Are you sure?"

"Yes," I said, pushing myself up and then nearly toppling over.

Callum put a supporting hand out, which I grabbed. I felt safe once again, but also incurably stupid. "Maybe I'll take you up on that ride," I managed to mumble. "If you're sure you can knock off from work without getting fired."

"I'll risk it."

We headed out the rear exit to Callum's beat-up old Honda, and I directed him the few blocks to my house. Along the way, I had to muster every ounce of strength to stop my hands from shaking.

"Thanks," I said when we'd pulled up to the curb. My breathing had slowed by now, and I'd begun to feel foolish for being so afraid of a well-dressed woman in a public park. What exactly could she have done to me, anyhow? "I'm sorry I'm such a mess. It's stupid, I know, to run away from someone like that."

"It's not stupid," he said, the words low and quiet. "You followed your instincts. Never second-guess yourself in times of crisis. Do you hear me?"

I narrowed my eyes at him. The way he spoke once again

made him sound like he'd had way more life experience than a seventeen-year-old should.

"I'll take that advice," I said.

"Good."

My hand reached for the car door handle, though I hesitated to open it. Doing so would mean walking away from Callum, and I didn't know when the next time was that we'd see each other.

"Tonight," he said, reading my mind again. "I'll be there. I'll be keeping an eye out for you."

I gawked at him, puzzled by his seeming interest in me. Why would a boy who was so impressive, so intriguing, so…different from any other boy I'd ever met…keep an eye out for a girl like me? The park would be teeming with far more interesting people tonight. If I wasn't a nobody in his eyes now, I'd definitely be one by then.

"Why would you watch for me?" I laughed.

"For many reasons. Not the least of which is that you're beautiful. I'd be a fool not to keep an eye out for you—even if you choose to cover your lovely face with a mask."

I opened my mouth to say something self-deprecating but decided against it. I supposed that one of these days I should finally learn to take a compliment.

Fighting back the desire to put myself down, I opened the door and climbed out before turning and leaning into the door frame. "Thank you, Callum," I said with an awkward smile.

"You're welcome," he replied.

As I watched his car accelerate down the street, an unfamiliar ache found its way into my chest, an unwelcome sense of hollowness. It was like a part of me had been torn away with Callum's departure.

Great. I was already falling for the boy with the bright eyes, and I'd only just met him.

"Careful, Vega," I said under my breath as I headed up the walkway toward my house. "Just be careful."

WHEN I'D MADE my way into the house, I trudged up to my second-floor bedroom. I unzipped my pocket and reached inside, hoping to find that the entire incident in the park had been a figment of my imagination. But when my fingers wrapped themselves around the strange key Charlie had given me, I winced. Part of me had hoped I'd only imagined it into existence, that it was all part of some intricate hallucination brought on by some dormant psychosis, or, preferably, by my lack of breakfast.

Reluctantly, I drew the key out of my pocket and stared at it for a moment before meandering over to the mirror next to my closet. After a moment of contemplation, I pulled the silver chain my grandmother had sent me out from under my collar and reached around for the clasp. But as I pulled gently at the chain, no clasp revealed itself. I kept yanking until I was certain I'd done at least two full rotations, inspecting every inch of the chain. It seemed impossible, but somehow, it had fused itself into one long, slinking silver coil around my neck.

"But how am I supposed to..." I muttered, holding the key up to see if there was some sort of mechanism on its back I could use to fasten it.

Even as I did this, the dangling chain lifted itself, pulling toward the key as though some powerful magnetic force had sparked to life inside it. Before I knew it, the key was hanging from my neck, the chain looped through one of its small openings.

On a whim I wrapped my fingers around the key and pulled. It came away easily in my hand, but by some miracle, the chain remained intact.

Once again, I brought the key close to the chain, and the two bonded in the same way as they had the first time. It was the strangest, most baffling magic trick I'd ever seen, and apparently, I was the one who'd performed it.

"What have you gotten me into, Nana?" I asked before tucking the key inside my shirt.

All of a sudden, I felt exhausted. Too much had happened. My brain was on overdrive, and I needed a rest. I spun around, marched across the room, and threw myself down onto my bed. Flipping onto my back, I tossed my arm over my eyes, shutting out the daylight.

"Enough. Enough with this freaking day."

WILL

I DRIFTED INTO A LONG, DEEP SLEEP.

After a time, I began to dream I was walking down a forest path, a light beckoning me in the distance. I strolled toward it, calm but wary, my pace picking up as a feeling of foreboding began to overtake me. As I advanced, the trees began closing in, looking to trap me between their oppressive limbs.

I picked up my pace to a jog, trying to escape the feeling of claustrophobia. The sound of baying wolves began to call out from behind me. I broke into a jog, then a full-out run, but the ominous canine shrieking only grew louder and louder. Terrified, I sprinted toward the source of light in the distance, breathing a sigh of relief when I spotted the outline of a large stone structure rising up before me. I could see towers, parapets —a massive, looming castle that looked like something out of the Middle Ages. White flags flew atop the turrets, displaying a symbol I couldn't quite make out.

I ran as fast as I could, aching to escape the encroaching woods. I was desperate to get to the castle and find shelter from the wolves, who were so close behind me now I could feel the heat of their breath on my heels. I could smell their damp fur, hear their paws strike the ground with the force of a hundred iron mallets. I tore ahead, knowing if they caught up with me, I'd be torn to shreds.

A hard, shrill cry from somewhere high overhead drew my eyes upwards. At first glance it looked as though a large bird was circling the woods, its expansive wings spread like sails filling half the sky above the treetops. But as I dashed ahead and the trees gave way to a large clearing leading to the castle, the flying creature began its descent toward me. Relief filled me like a drug. Something told me the bird was there to help, to drive away the wolves and carry me to safety.

But when the creature came crashing to earth, its massive talons digging into the hard ground, I screamed. The flying beast was no bird. It was a dragon, and its mouth was cracking open to reveal white-hot sparks bursting to life at the back of its throat.

I was caught between two enemies. One would tear me to pieces, the other would burn me into a lump of coal.

It was up to me to decide which way I would die.

THE MUFFLED SOUND of a male voice stirred me from sleep and saved me from dying in my dream. Disoriented and clammy with sweat, I rolled over and fumbled for my phone, the intense dream fading mercifully into wisps of fragmented images.

"Damn," I said as I stared at the screen. "Four o'clock. How could you let me sleep that long?" I asked. Thankfully, the phone didn't answer me.

As memories of the morning's bizarre events and my harrowing nightmare came flooding back, my heart began to race. But when I closed my eyes and focused on the sound of a cheerful young man singing to himself, a feeling of calm swept over me. A smile traced its way over my lips as I realized that the voice belonged to someone I'd missed all summer.

"Will!" I yelled out, leaping off the bed and out of my room. I sprinted down the stairs and into the kitchen where I threw myself into my brother's waiting arms. Laughing hysterically, he stumbled back against the counter as I crashed into him hard enough to shake the dishes drying in the silver rack by the sink.

"Jeez, Vega, I was wondering if you were going to sleep the whole time I was here!" he chuckled as he released me. He shot me an appraising look before adding, "You've gotten taller over the summer, you know."

"I still have a ways to go before I catch up to you," I laughed. Will was 6'1" and there was no way I was ever going to catch up to him—not that I particularly wanted to. More likely I'd be my mother's height—nice and average—which was fine with me.

"Listen, in honor of your birthday I'm ordering in tonight. But I want to make sure we're finished eating by seven so we can get ready."

"Ready?" I replied. "For what?"

"Midsummer Fest, silly," Will said, smacking me gently on the top of my head. "But we can skip it and do something else if you want."

"Ow!" I shouted, rubbing my head in mock agony. "You're really planning on going?"

A mix of excitement and apprehension worked its way through me. Attending the procession would mean the possibility of seeing Callum again. But it could also mean running into the horrid woman from the park.

"You *are* coming with me, right?" Will asked. "We never miss it."

"Um..." I replied, quickly conjuring an excuse. "I'm not really sure. I don't have a mask..."

"Of course you do. I got a little something for you on my travels." He reached for a large wrapped box sitting on the kitchen island. In my excitement at seeing him I hadn't even noticed it. "Happy Birthday, Sis."

My eyes bugged out as I held the large gift in my hands. I set it on the kitchen table and ripped it open, only to discover what looked like eighty layers of white tissue paper.

"Are you sure there's actually something in here?" I laughed. "I mean, not that I'm not grateful for such an awesome box of garbage."

"I'm sure. I had a heck of a time getting that thing onto the plane."

I reached into the box, rifling through the paper until my hand met something smooth and cool. Grabbing its edge, I eased it from the box, gasping when I set my eyes on it.

The object was a mask, pure white with a prominent nose, complete with nostrils and a set of feminine lips with a small hole, apparently for breathing.

But something about it wasn't quite right.

"There are no eyes," I said, a feeling of murky foreboding swirling through my mind as I stared at it. It wasn't only that the mask lacked holes where the eyes should have been. It didn't even have indentations to depict them. The face looked oppressive, blinding, like something that would imprison me inside itself. "Why aren't there eyes?"

"Read what it says on the back," Will said with a funny smile.

I did as he said, turning the mask over. Inside, in a tidy painted script, were the words,

Wear me and see all.

"Weird, right?" Will said as I stared. "I mean, that it's in English instead of Italian. I guess they expected an American tourist to buy it or something."

"Definitely weird."

Confused, I pulled the elastic strap attached to either side and glided the mask over my head to secure it in place. To my surprise, I could see Will as clearly as if I wasn't wearing anything over my eyes at all. In fact, if anything, his features looked clearer, more in focus somehow. I could see every pore on his nose, every bit of stubble coating his chin.

"This is wild," I said. "High-def vision! Where did it come from?"

"I was in Venice for a week," Will replied. "That place is famous for its masks. I mean, most of them are super-ornate, covered in decorations. Feathers, gold, you name it. I was about to buy you a black one with red feathers when this old woman in a shop stopped me."

"Wait," I said, pulling the mask off. "I've already had my fill of mysticism for the day. Is this going to be one of those stories you see in movies about old ladies selling cursed monkey paws?"

"Sort of," Will laughed. "She was a bit of a loon. She literally walked up to me holding this thing in her gnarled hand and said, 'You must give this face'—I remember specifically that she said 'face' and not 'mask'—'to your sister, the Seeker.'"

As he said the last word, I drew in a quick breath, nearly dropping the fragile mask. Reeling, I staggered away from Will.

"Wait—what did you just say?"

My face must have turned white, because he reached out and grabbed my arm to steady me. "Vega! You okay?"

I nodded. "Fine," I said. "Sorry. I must not have eaten enough today." I pulled myself up onto one of the kitchen's wooden stools. "Tell me—did she say anything else?"

Will looked pensive for a moment. "She said one thing—that the mask would 'teach the Seeker how to see the world as it truly is.' I asked her what that means, and she said 'It is not for you to know. But the Seeker will come to understand soon enough.' She was all mysterious and spooky about it. Honestly, it's probably just some silly sales pitch she uses to make the big bucks. I guess it worked, because there was no way I could say no after that. I just nodded and smiled, and handed her my cash."

"So weird," I said with a withering smile. "But thanks. It's... really amazing."

"I got a mask for myself, too," Will said, reaching into his large army surplus bag and pulling out a black papier-mâché creation. It was shiny, with two round eye holes and what looked like a giant beak. "They call it a Plague Doctor mask. People used to think these would keep them from getting sick. They said the long nose created a pocket of clean air doctors would breathe in, so they didn't catch the plague from the sick people they were helping."

"Did they work?" I asked skeptically. "The masks, I mean."

"I don't see too many doctors walking around with the plague, so I guess they must have."

"Cute," I said, my heart still hammering in my chest after Will's tale of the strange woman in Venice.

"Anyhow," he said, "you and me. The Festival. Tonight, after dinner. If you try to stay home, I'll drag you out by your hair."

"Try it and you'll get bit, big Brother."

Will laughed.

"Fine," I said, "I'll go. As long as you promise to stay with me."

"Stay with you?" he asked with a look of surprise. "Of course I will. But Vega—you look kind of freaked out. Are you okay?"

I eyed him for a moment, chewing the inside of my cheek before saying, "You're going to think I've lost it."

"I won't. Promise."

I told him about our grandmother's gift of the necklace and Charlie handing me the box containing the strange dragon key. Even as I did so, I felt all the apprehension that had built up over the day melting away. Somehow, saying the words out loud made the two incidents seem less shocking.

"And see?" I said, drawing the dragon key and chain out from under my shirt. "They link together." Will watched as I demonstrated the magic trick where the key connected to the chain, locked on somehow, and then slipped off when I tugged it a certain way.

"Probably magnets," Will suggested, leaning in to inspect the key and the chain more closely. "Either way, it's pretty neat."

"So, what do you think? Does it mean something, or am I losing it?"

"Well, Nana's always been weird, as you know, so I wouldn't worry about any of that. As for Charlie's present...maybe it was his way of thanking you for always being nice to him. You're one of the few people who is, you know."

"Maybe," I said. I still hadn't told him about the woman in the park, about the odd way she'd looked at me, or how she'd acted like she'd come to Fairhaven just to find me. I still wasn't quite convinced I hadn't imagined the whole thing.

"I'm glad you're here," I added. "Oh, by the way, Liv will be at Midsummer Fest and I promised we'd look for her. You'd better be prepared. I think she's planning to propose to you tonight."

"Great," Will said, grabbing me in a headlock with one arm, grabbing the mask with the other hand, and dragging me toward the stairs. "I'll be sure to turn her down gently. But don't worry about all the other stuff—it sounds like you just had a weird day. Besides, you got some nice new jewelry out of it." He released me at the bottom of the staircase and smiled. "I know it's just until tomorrow, but man, it's good to be back in Fairhaven."

"It's good to have you home," I said, punching his arm.

By the time I made it upstairs, I'd all but forgotten the madness that had befallen me that morning.

Will was home, and nothing else mattered.

MIDSUMMER FEST

AT 8:00 P.M., AFTER WE'D EATEN DINNER AND SCARFED DOWN TWO cinder-block sized pieces of a double-chocolate cake Will had picked up at our local bakery, we found ourselves walking through Norfolk Commons' main gates. Will was dressed in his long-beaked plague doctor mask, a pair of blue jeans, and a faded gray sweater with the sleeves pushed up to his elbows.

I'd changed into charcoal-gray jeans, a black t-shirt, and a black hoodie with the strange white mask Will had given me covering my face.

"You look like the Angel of Death," he told me as we walked along.

"Good," I replied. "Maybe it'll keep people from talking to me. I just wish I'd thought to bring that scythe from the garage. That would have completed the look *and* kept everyone at a respectful distance."

"Come on now. You know the rules for Midsummer Fest," Will said, ticking them off one at a time on his fingers with pretend sternness. "No alcohol. No drugs. No unleashed pets. No bare feet. And absolutely no long-handled, razor-sharp weapons of mass decapitation."

"That's the problem with these big public parties," I said, giving Will a playful nudge with my elbow. "They get you all geared up but then never let you have any real fun."

"Hurry up, Miss Death!" he urged, breaking into a jog. "I want to have a look at everyone's hideous faces."

It seemed most of the town had gathered in the park already by the time we arrived. Groups of teenagers were huddled here and there, laughing at one another's costumes and masks. The younger kids bounced and yipped all over each other, while the older kids played it cool, bantering back and forth, talking politics, and telling dirty jokes.

I swung around to see if I could locate Callum, half expecting to spot him talking to Miranda Smythe, Plymouth High's prettiest—and most evil—senior. I was no fan of hers, or of the "Charmers," which was the name Liv and I had given the small but cruel cult-like clique of snooty girls who worshipped her as some kind of snarky deity.

The idea of Callum getting sucked into their vortex of haughty stupidity would have broken my heart. He didn't strike me as the sort to fall for the prom-queen type, but then, what did I know about relationships? I'd never had a boyfriend. My first kiss was a disastrous incident that unfolded during a game of spin the bottle at a party at Liv's when I was thirteen. As everyone oohed and ahhed, I leaned in to meet Kevin Lewandowski over the glass soda bottle only to have him shriek in pain when my braces sliced a deep gash in his lower lip. He spent the rest of the night in the bathroom with a piece of gauze pressed to his mouth.

At least that's what I heard. I didn't witness the aftermath, as I was too busy running home, crying and lava-hot with embarrassment.

That turned me off of kissing for a while, and I don't think it did much to inspire Kevin, either.

As I searched the crowd for Callum, my gaze moved through

the throngs of noisy people. Most of the costumes were relatively innocuous: a white rabbit here, a black, Zorro-like half-mask there. After a little while, I found my eyes drawn to the face of a teenage girl I'd never seen before. She wasn't wearing a mask, which may have been why she stood out among the raucous menagerie. But there was something odd about her, too.

Her skin was a milky, almost translucent white. Her eyes were emerald green, and her mane of hair was a spectrum of thick, wavy browns. But what was most striking about her was the animal draped around her neck like a scarf. At first, I thought she was wearing a mink stole, but after a few seconds, it moved, slithering over her shoulders like a furry snake. The image sent a chill into my bones, up my spine, and through my teeth. I wasn't usually squeamish, but the events of the day had me on edge.

Next to the girl was a young man without a mask whose face was deeply scarred by one long, red slash mark along his right cheek. He looked like he'd been on the losing end of a knife fight. He and the girl were huddled close, engaged in what looked like an intense conversation, when they were approached by a tall young man with broad shoulders and the most expressive blue eyes I'd ever seen.

"Callum," I mouthed silently, a smile stretching my lips wide.

In his right hand, pinched between his thumb and his first two fingers, he held what looked like a dragon mask. He twirled it absently as he talked with the green-eyed girl and the scarred boy, who both shot me quiet glances across the park's jogging path as if they were sizing me up. I looked away, pretending not to notice them—and hoping my mask was enough to conceal my interest.

As I was peeking back at them out of the corner of my eye, the girl nodded to the boy, and the furry animal around her neck raised its head and glared at me through black, slightly sinister-looking eyes.

"What the heck are you staring at?" Will asked.

Flustered, I pulled my mask off and looked at him for a second. His eyes sparkled behind the plague doctor mask, and I could tell he was smiling.

"I just..." I began, "there's a girl with an animal over there. A ferret, I think. Maybe a mink. I don't really know the difference. I was sort of mesmerized, I guess."

"Where?" Will asked, looking around.

"Where what?"

"Where's the ferret?"

"Over there," I replied, glancing as inconspicuously as possible toward Callum's trio. They were still standing together, still talking...but the ferret had disappeared.

"I don't see a ferret," Will said.

"Neither do I. It must have slipped into her bag or something."

Confused, I pulled my mask back on and took another look at the girl. As I stared, the ferret reappeared, jutting its small head out and staring at me again with an eerie, piercing kind of awareness.

"Um, Will," I said quietly, turning to my brother.

"Hmm?"

Without taking my eyes off the ferret—or whatever it was—I tugged on Will's sleeve. "The woman in Venice—the one with the masks...did she say anything about this one making people see weird things?"

"Weird things? Like what?"

"Like evil-eyed but adorable rodents."

Will let out a laugh and waggled his fingers in the air in front of his face. "Oooo...are you hallucinating?"

"Knock it off," I said with a hard smack to his arm. "I'm serious."

"Ow," he said, holding his upper arm like he'd been shot. "There's nothing sinister about the mask, and, before you ask, no, I didn't slip any psychotropic drugs into your milk."

"That's great," I said. "So, I'm just losing my mind."

"You always did have a great imagination, Sis."

Ignoring Will, I took one last glance at the trio, catching Callum's eye for a second. It was so strange—I knew he couldn't see my eyes through my expressionless mask, but somehow, I still felt like he was looking right into them.

After a few seconds he put a hand on the shoulder of each of his two companions before moving away with them into the crowd.

Hearing someone call out, "Vega!" I whipped around to see a giant zebra head weaving its way through the jostling crowd and heading right toward me and Will.

"There you are!" Liv yelled, her voice deep and muffled from inside the striped rubber head. "Cool mask, Vega. I wouldn't have known it was you except for the fact that I recognized your satchel." She turned to my brother, hopping up and down, her hands clasped together. "Will," she chirped, "you look so handsome, even in that weird bird-head!" She threw her arms around him, hugging so tight he let out a choked cough.

"Thanks, I think," he chuckled, pushing her gently away.

"Come on," Liv commanded. "We need to get our candles and noise-makers! The procession starts in a few minutes."

We made our way over to a long table where for two dollars Liv and Will each purchased a red plastic kazoo and a glass containing a white candle to carry with them on the procession.

"You're not getting one?" Liv asked me, holding up her candle.

I shook my head. "Nah. I want my hands free in case..." I stopped myself, realizing there was no way to finish the thought without giving away what had happened earlier in the day. I wasn't about to explain that I might need my hands to punch some stranger in the face. "I just don't want to set myself on fire," I said.

"That's okay," Liv giggled, throwing an arm around my shoulders. "If you want, you can share mine."

When we'd moved back into the long line of festival attendees, a voice crackled over a nearby speaker announcing the procession was about to begin. "Happy Midsummer Fest!" it screeched. "May the remainder of summer be momentous and remarkable for you all!"

Liv elbowed me gently in the side, nodding up ahead. "Ugh, look who's talking to the Charmers," she whisper-hissed. Our three enemies were standing off to the side, talking to Callum, who was in the process of slipping his dragon mask over his head. My heart sank with the realization that the very meeting I'd been dreading was taking place right before my eyes.

"I heard Miranda's been trying to sink her press-on claws into Callum ever since he moved to town," Liv said. "Not surprising, but still super-irritating."

As I watched him, Callum turned and shot me a look, his blue eyes flashing behind the large, angry-looking eyeholes of his mask. His irises flared under the last rays of the setting sun so that, just for a second, they looked as though they were glowing gold before shifting back to that icy ocean blue.

Callum nodded and stepped away from the Charmers, and before I knew it, he'd tucked himself somewhere up ahead in the pack. I couldn't help feeling hurt that he hadn't come over to say "Hi" after what had happened between us earlier. Then again, maybe he'd just been playing with my mind for kicks. Maybe he was the kind of guy who thought it was fun to tell a girl she was beautiful and then blow her off.

"Vega? You okay?" Will asked, taking hold of my arm as we shuffled along with the rowdy crowd.

Snap out of it, I told myself. *You just met the guy today. It's not like he's your boyfriend.*

"Fine," I lied. "I'm fine."

"Come on, let's do this!" Liv said, tucking herself between Will and me and hooking her arms into ours. It was nice having her next to me. Her presence made me feel like the world had at least retained some element of normalcy after all of today's wackiness.

The crowd pushed forward down the road between the yellow police barriers lining the jogging path in the park. Our candles lit the way as the sun finished its descent and the moon rose high over the Commons. After a time, a chorus somewhere within the crowd began to belt out a traditional song written for the procession. I'd never really paid attention to the lyrics, but for some reason, this time I forced myself to listen, especially after one verse in particular caught my attention:

Midsummer comes, the dragons wake,
The lands begin to shift
New doors open to the world of old
As the Seeker gains her gift

I nearly stopped in my tracks, stunned to hear the word *Seeker* —a word I must have heard every year at Midsummer Fest without ever registering it. I turned to Will, who was busy listening to Liv recount a radically embellished story about catching what sounded like a very small fish at the cottage with her father.

What does it mean? I wondered. *The Seeker gains her gift? What gift, exactly? And what was that line about the dragons?*

I tried to make out the rest of the lyrics, which were mostly about the coming of falling leaves, music, and something to do with wind. None of them gave me any hints as to what a Seeker was, or just why I'd been given the key.

We walked until we made our way out of the park, then proceeded down High Street. Residents of Fairhaven who weren't participating in the procession had come to watch and were lining the street on either side.

We'd just wandered past The Novel Hovel when I spotted a set of dark eyes to my left. A tall, thin man with black hair was staring at me, his fingers balled into menacing fists. I recognized him immediately as the groundskeeper who'd waved at me when Liv and I walked past the park that morning. As we passed him, I turned around to see him tucking himself into the procession behind us.

To my right, Liv was busily asking Will questions about every topic imaginable. What courses he planned to take at college, how often he'd be coming home, if he was living in residence, how likely it was that he'd remain single for the next four years. As room on the street grew narrower, I pulled up to walk behind them, smiling quietly to myself as I studied their body language. Will was keeping his distance, but Liv kept sidling up right next to him as though hoping for a little accidental contact. I almost wanted to put her out of her misery by offering to set her up on a date with some guy or other. If only I actually knew any boys. I would have suggested Kevin Lewandowski; after all, he was smart and cute. But he hadn't spoken to me or made eye contact since our little spin-the-bottle disaster.

So, instead of contemplating potential mates to distract my hyper-amorous friend, I found myself looking over my shoulder as we walked, searching for the dark-haired man in the crowd. At one point I saw him, his ghostly face standing out among a sea of masks, his dark eyes oddly luminous under the pale street lamps.

By the time I turned back, I'd lost Will and Liv in the jostling crowd. I was about to leap forward through the revelers and try to catch up when a car pulled out of a driveway in front of me, blocking my path.

It was so close, I had to put my hand on the hood of the car and skip back to avoid being hit. When it had pulled out again, I picked up my pace, pushing forward to try to locate Will and Liv. I'd just come to the narrow alley between the bakery and the travel agency when a hand clamped down hard on my shoulder and dragged me to the side. Thrown off balance, I staggered into the alley, my hands reaching for the brick walls to either side in an attempt to steady myself. I spun around, cursing my mask for cutting off my peripheral vision.

Right in front of me was the dark-haired man whose black eyes were staring into my own, though I knew all he could see was an eyeless white face staring back at him.

The man's face contorted as he edged toward me, his lips curling down into a savage, canine snarl as a low, animalistic grumble emerged from deep inside his chest.

"What do you want?" I asked, reaching inside my satchel, hoping to find something I could use as a weapon. My fingers curled around a tube of lip gloss and two packs of gum but nothing deadly enough to scare anyone off. *Damn it. Now I really wish I'd brought that scythe from the garage.*

"You have something," the man said, his voice raspy and low. "Something I need." He moved toward me, pushing me deeper into the alley. I couldn't run at him. He was too big for me to knock over, and besides, who knew what he'd do if he got his hands on me?

I shouted at him to back off, but he didn't budge, so I yelled again, this time louder, hoping someone on the street would hear me and come help. But by now, the Midsummer Fest parade had shifted into overdrive with hundreds of people singing, calling out to each other, and blasting out thundering rhythms on an orchestra of tambourines, kazoos, and kettle drums.

I realized with a sinking sense of doom that my next best option was to run all the way down the alley until I came out on the other side. If I could just make it to the other end, I might be able to get away from this psycho and find help.

"Look, I don't know what you're talking about," I said, backpedaling and looking the man in the eye. I had to work hard to keep my voice steady while I backed slowly away, deeper into the narrow alleyway. "I don't know who you are."

"Who I am doesn't matter. I know who you are, Vega Sloane," he said. "I know *what* you are."

"Well," I half-laughed, "that makes one of us."

Before he could take another step toward me, I spun around and sprinted down the alley, running as fast as I could through an obstacle course of garbage cans, wooden skids, and a line of overturned shopping carts. But as fast as I was sprinting through the dark, the man's rapid, heavy footsteps pounded right behind me, getting louder and closer with each step. I bolted, my eyes locked on the bright spot of light at the end of the alleyway up ahead.

After twenty or so seconds, I began to wonder how it was that the brick walls were still rising up on either side of me. By now I should have freed myself from the oppressive, narrow corridor and hit the street at the opposite end. But the alley seemed to grow longer as I ran. Even stranger, a thin mist had begun swirling around my feet, turning quickly into a dense fog.

As I tore along, losing sight of my own feet, the walls to my left and right disintegrated. In their place, thick, arching trees appeared, imprisoning me beneath their limbs. The scent of wet leaves hung in the air. All around me, shadows appeared, swayed, and disappeared like panthers preparing to pounce. Reeling, I pushed forward, willing this all too familiar nightmare to end... and praying it wouldn't end in my death.

Bursting from the fog, I slid to an abrupt stop at a large wooden door that was blocking my way. The thick, impenetrable barrier was ornately carved with the twisting neck of an immense, fire-breathing dragon.

With my throat raw and tears of terror welling up in my eyes, I slapped my palms against the door and then tried pounding on it with the sides of my fists.

It didn't budge.

Whipping around, I saw the man slow to an easy jog and then to a determined stride, confident he'd trapped me at last.

I spun back to the door, my eyes locking onto a large keyhole, glowing like a lighthouse beacon in a storm. Without thinking and acting on a combination of instinct and pure adrenaline, I snatched the dragon-headed key off the chain around my neck and thrust the silver shaft into the lock. I was already congratulating myself for my quick thinking when a pair of powerful hands grabbed my shoulders and yanked me backwards.

I watched in horror as the door vanished into the mist and the key fell to the ground with a sickening clang.

WAERG

I TWISTED AROUND TO CONFRONT MY ATTACKER, READY TO SCREAM. To fight. My pulse pounded in my temples. My stomach seized into a rigid knot. A million scenarios—none of them good—flashed through my mind about how this might go. All I knew was that I had to survive. I might not have had the greatest life ever, but it was my life, and I wasn't ready for it to end.

Give me one more chance, I prayed to the universe and to whatever guiding force might be out there. *One more chance to see Will. To see Liv. To see Callum, too. I promise to do better. To be better. Just please, please, please let me out of this.*

But my prayers went unanswered.

The man swung me around, pushing me hard against the alley wall. Every instinct I had to run fizzled away to be replaced by a strange paralysis. It wasn't fear. More like I was frozen, hypnotized.

Unable to move, I had no choice but to look into the face of the man glaring fire at me.

Only he wasn't a man.

Not anymore.

Staring into my eyes was a monstrous gray wolf, its lips

pulled back in a snarl, its teeth jagged and razor-sharp. The fur on its back and shoulders bristled, its back legs coiled under its broad body as it prepared to pounce.

Tearing off my mask, I leaned back against the cold brick wall, my hands open and extended in front of me. My heart and lungs tightened with horror, tears burning in my eyes at the thought of being ripped apart and eaten alive. But as the mask fell to the ground from my trembling fingers, the wolf—in less than the space of an eye-blink—morphed back into the man who'd been chasing me. In the place of a mouth full of sharp teeth was a set of dry, thin lips. In the place of a long muzzle and fur were creased skin, a crooked nose, and eyes as black and cold as a rag doll's.

My throat went raw. My eyes were stinging and wet. Either I was dreaming, seeing things, or else I'd gone completely insane. "What do you want?" I stammered through a trickle of tears.

My pursuer pulled his eyes to the ground behind me, focusing on the spot where the dragon key lay shining in the darkness by my heel. "Mistress sent me for it," he said in a voice more animal than human. "Mistress says you must not find them...You must be stopped."

"Leave me alone!" I shot back, a lump forming in my throat.

"Give it to me," he said with a nod toward the ground at my feet. "Offer it to me, and I will accept."

"Fine," I stammered, twisting around to pick the key up and thrusting my arm toward him. "Take it!"

He started to hold out his hand but jerked it back.

"Here! Take it!" Anger was bubbling up inside me now, feeding on my fear. I hated feeling so vulnerable, so helpless.

But instead of taking the dragon key and leaving me alone, the man dropped his eyes and shook his head. "I can't."

I chucked the key to the ground at his feet and started to step away. "You wanted it. It's all yours. Just leave me alone."

The sinister look in my stalker's eyes softened as he knelt down and cupped his hands around the key without touching it.

"I can't accept it if it's given out of fear. The Old Magic doesn't allow it."

"Then we're in for a long night, Buddy," I stammered. "Because fear is pretty much all I've got right now." As I stared at him, the sudden realization flashed through my mind that he could have easily shoved me out of the way, grabbed the key, and bolted. But he just knelt there, looking back and forth between me and the dirty ground where the key sat, glinting in the yellow light cast down by the moon high above us.

"Look," I said, inching along the wall toward the far end of the alley. "You wanted the key. It's yours. My brother is right down there in the parade. I'm going to get back to him, and you can have your *Precious,* and go terrorize someone else for a while."

"You should never have been given such a gift," the man snarled, his face returning to a knot of crumpled rage as the wolf's features flashed across his own. "You don't know anything about the lands beyond the Breach." He stood up again and stepped back, his chin tilted down so he was glaring at me through the tops of his eyes.

"You're right," I said. "I don't know anything about lands or breaches. But I promise to read all about them as soon as I get home."

As the man gave me a puzzled, head-scratching stare, a strange thought occurred to me: I should want the key as far away from me as possible. But something about it was drawing me in, and something about the man's reaction told me the small trinket might offer the protection or leverage I might need in case he changed his mind and decided to come after me again. Hesitant, but drawn forward by a force beyond anything in my mind or body, I knelt down in front of the man, my eyes never wavering from his. With my fingers shaking, I picked up the key and held it next to the chain around my neck, where the two pieces of jewelry bound themselves protectively together, the chain embracing its partner by whatever bizarre magnetism made it work.

"Look," I said, standing back up with a sudden glimmer of confidence. "I don't know what you really want from me. But I do know that you're a psycho, and I'm looking forward to seeing the cops come back here and taze your creepy ass back to whatever hole you crawled out of. I don't know why I didn't phone them the moment I set eyes on you." Reaching into my back pocket but never taking my eyes off of my would-be assailant, I slipped my cell phone out, glanced down, and pressed the button that brought the screen to life.

But before I could dial, the fog around us dissipated, and the brick walls of the two buildings on either side of the alley reappeared. I didn't know what was happening, only that I could hear the parade again.

Will had to be close by now.

So why did I still feel like I was about to die?

Without warning, the man lunged at me as though he intended to rip my throat out, his hands reaching for my neck, clawing like the paws of a wild animal fighting for its life. "You should not have the dragon's key!" he shrieked. "You cannot be worthy of it!"

I leapt backwards, my phone skittering under a palette of wooden skids. Tripping over a break in the uneven surface of the dark alleyway, I fell with a heavy thud, and in a flash the man was on me again, gripping the neckline of my hoodie in his hard, bony fists and hauling me to my feet. I grabbed at his wrists, trying desperately to wrench him off, but he was too strong. I kicked at his legs as hard as I could, but he shrugged off my attack and slammed me hard against the alley wall. My head cracked against the jagged bricks, and nausea overtook me as I felt the heat of blood trickling down my neck. I crumpled to the ground, my body giving out under the shock.

With a cluster of aluminum garbage cans on one side of me, a blue recycling dumpster on the other, and the menacing man looming in front of me, I was totally cornered.

The man took a step backwards, a twisted smile on his lips as he cocked his head to the side like a curious dog.

Determined not to die in that alley, I'd just begun to scramble to my feet when a deep voice from behind the man bellowed, "Get away from her!"

I looked up past my enemy to see a pair of blue eyes piercing through the darkness, reflecting the dim light like a cat's. A tall figure walked toward us, a dragon mask in his right hand.

"Callum?" I breathed.

"Did he hurt you, Vega?"

I shook my head. "What? No. I mean, not really."

"Good." Callum shouldered past the man to help me to my feet before turning back to take an intimidating wide-legged stance between us. "Leave," he ordered. "You don't belong here, *Waerg*. You know it. And your mistress knows it. She was wrong to send you."

"You don't speak for my mistress, Callum Drake." The words came out like the guttural warning of a feral animal. The sound was so shocking it didn't even occur to me in the moment to question how the stranger knew Callum's name. "She sent me here for a reason."

"I'm here for a reason, too," Callum said, an unmistakable threat peppering his voice. "And your reason and my reason aren't going to get along too well."

I could hear the crack and pop of Callum's knuckles as he clenched his hands into fists at his sides.

The man hesitated for a moment then tried to leap at me again, but as he did, Callum intercepted him, grabbed him by the collar and shoved him so hard against the alley wall I swore the ground shook beneath my feet. A spray of dust and pieces of brick blasted into the air.

"Touch her again, wolf-kin, and I'll kill you right here," Callum hissed, his face an inch away from the other man's.

Cowed, the man nodded, the whites of his eyes glowing in the darkness. A toxic mist of fear clouded his face, and he whimpered like a frightened dog.

Finally, Callum released him. The man recoiled in horror, shrinking into a small, curled up ball on the ground against the wall. "You don't have the right," he sniveled. "Mistress says..."

"Your mistress is a usurper, and you're an infiltrator," Callum snapped. "You know the rules. You can't come here and take what belongs to a Seeker. I'm seriously tempted to burn your worthless body to ash."

With my breath locked tight in my chest, I stood there, my back pressed against the wall behind Callum, fingers grasping at the bricks as I tried to will the nightmare to end.

Had Callum, the gentle, friendly boy I'd met this morning, really just threatened to murder someone?

"No, please," the man replied, slouching in submission. "Please?"

Callum looked over his shoulder at me before turning back to the cowering man. "If I see you in Fairhaven again," he growled, "I'll summon *him*, and you'll die. You and your Waerg companions. Do you understand me?"

Staring at the ground, the man nodded, his hair damp with sweat.

"Callum..." I whispered, unable to fully engage my speaking voice.

He turned my way, his expression softening when he saw the look on my face.

"Who...who is he?" I asked. "*What* is he?"

"You already know. You've seen it."

I shook my head so violently it hurt. "No, I really don't know anything at all. I don't understand any of this."

"Tell me, what did you see when you looked at him with your mask on?"

"I saw an animal," I replied, my voice trembling. "A wolf. But I...I was only imagining it."

"Look again." Callum picked up the white mask from where I had dropped it near one of the garbage cans. His fingers brushed against mine as he handed it to me, just as they'd done in the bookshop that morning. The tingle of his touch made me fear that this—all of it—was real. "Put it on."

Still hypnotized with terror and confused down to my bones, I pressed the mask to my face and looked through the non-existent eyes. All of a sudden, the man was gone, and in his place was the same gray wolf I'd seen a minute ago.

Well, *almost* the same.

The fierceness had left his eyes. He looked mangy. His fur was matted and dirty. His irises were dark, and his belly was pressed low to the ground. What moments ago looked like a terrifying beast now seemed pathetic, weakened to the point of near-death.

Baffled, I tore the mask off again, and the creature slowly morphed into the dark-haired man, now shivering against the alley wall.

Callum stepped forward to stand over him. "Niala! Crow!" he called out into the cold gloom.

Two silent figures emerged from the shadows beyond Callum: the girl I'd seen with the ferret on her shoulder, and the boy with the scar. At Callum's feet, the defeated man pushed himself up, his head sunk low, seemingly resigned to his fate.

"Get him out of here," Callum commanded to the two newcomers. "Have him sent back to *her* with a warning not to interfere again. The Trials will take place soon enough. After that, she can do what she wants."

Both the girl and the boy nodded, and as I watched, the ferret leapt down off the girl's shoulder and landed in a quiet crouch on the alley floor where it transformed instantly into a large black panther, golden eyes glinting in its shadowy face.

The large black cat let out a low growl as Callum's two friends grabbed my assailant's arms and pulled him down the alley away from me. The panther padded after them, its muscles rippling in the dappled light.

"What's happening?" I asked. "Why did he look like that? Why did that girl's ferret turn into a panther?" I flipped the mask around in my hands. "What the hell *is* this thing?"

Callum reached out and slipped his fingers under my chin, pulling my face up toward his. "You turned seventeen today," he said. "You're starting to discover your gifts."

I waved my hand down the alley in the direction Callum's two friends, their pet panther, and the psycho man-dog mugger had just gone. "This? This is a gift?"

"More than you know."

"Couldn't you just have gotten me a card?"

Callum chuckled, a boyish smile playing at the corners of his mouth. "This birthday will see you getting gifts beyond anything you thought possible."

"And probably ones I won't want, right?"

"Well," he drawled, suddenly serious. "In this case, what you want isn't as important as what you *are*."

"And what am I, exactly?"

When Callum didn't answer, I shook my head and brushed the dirt from my hands. "I feel like I'm losing my mind," I said, shaking my head as I fought back tears. "I've seen the strangest things today…I really need to get back to Will…and Liv…"

"You're not losing your mind. And you're not alone. There are others who understand." Callum nodded back in the direction the man and his two captors had gone. "*They* understand. Crow and Niala are friends of mine."

I was shaking, my fingers cold, my legs trembling and weak.

"Who are you, Callum? Really. And how, exactly, did you manage to drug me?"

Callum's eyes danced, and he let out a rich, baritone laugh. "You're not drugged. I promise. In fact, what's happening to you is kind of the opposite of being drugged. Drugs obscure the truth. Today has been all about introducing you to the truth behind what everyone else calls reality."

"Reality? Ha!" I scoffed. "This has been the most surreal experience of my life. Even you—you don't seem real, Callum."

"Me? I'm just a guy who's trying to protect you."

"That's great," I said, running my hand along the back of my neck and inspecting my fingertips for traces of blood. "Do you think you can protect me about five minutes earlier next time?"

Callum looked shocked for a second before he seemed to realize I was joking. "I'm not so sure you're going to need my protection for long," he said. "You summoned a Breach. That takes serious strength."

I must have had a full page of confusion written on my face because he stopped and took a breath. "You didn't get a chance to look at the book, did you?" he asked.

"Book?" I replied. Even as I said the word, my jaw dropped open. "The book you gave me this morning," I said. "Before the incident in the park..." I wanted to kick myself. "Oh, no. I must have left it on the park bench after I opened Charlie's gift. I was so confused..."

Callum let out a strange chuckle. "It's all right. It was nothing important. Just...your invitation into another realm. That's all."

"I'm going to pretend I understand what that means, even though I totally don't," I said. "But you said I summoned a Breach?"

"You did, yes. A Breach is like a door. Only not just anyone can summon it, and very few can walk through. The calling up of a Breach...it causes a ripple effect in our reality. It's how I knew where to find you—and it's how I knew you were the person I'd hoped you were."

"And who's that, exactly?"

He reached out and tapped the dragon-shaped pendant dangling from my neck. "This key of yours? The one that's been causing you so much trouble? It means you've been recruited by the Academy for the Blood-Born. Well, the key and the book that you so cleverly misplaced."

I let out something midway between a laugh and a sob. "Excuse me?" I asked. "*Recruited?*"

Callum shot a look toward the street, where a few people were milling around at the entrance to the alley.

"Look," he said, "I want to tell you everything. Really, I do. But this day—as you know—has gone terribly wrong. I was supposed to help you. To get you the book, to steer you in the direction of the Academy. Unfortunately, it would seem there are some pretty powerful people who consider you dangerous and don't want you there."

"Oh, sure," I grunted. "A psychotic wolf-man attacks me in an alley, and *I'm* the dangerous one."

"You might be surprised, actually."

"I don't think so," I shot out. "Listen, I don't know who you're really looking for, but I'm pretty sure you have the wrong girl, Callum."

He shook his head. "You're wrong. I definitely have the right girl." With that, he reached out and pulled me toward him.

Oh my God, I thought. *He's...he's going to kiss me. Well, I guess one kiss wouldn't exactly be unpleasant. A kiss goodbye, then we'll never see each other again.*

But whatever fantasy I might have entertained about being swept off my feet by a knight in shining armor was put on hold as he turned me gently around, brushed my hair to one side, and inspected the cut on the back of my head.

"It's nothing," he announced with the clinical distance of a pediatrician telling a worried mother that her kid just had a minor cold. Callum pulled a small wad of white napkins from his pocket and pressed them against the cut. "Don't worry," he assured me. "They're clean. Hold this here. It'll be healed before you know it. Damn it, I should have asked Niala to look at you. She's way better at this sort of thing than I am."

Turning me back around, he touched my face again, his fingers slipping along my right cheek. I closed my eyes and embraced the sensation of being alive and safe, grateful to feel something other than fear.

"Go find your brother," Callum murmured, pulling away after a moment. "Find Liv. Enjoy the rest of the parade and your birthday. No one will be coming after you again, at least not tonight. I promise. As for the Academy, we'll talk some more tomorrow. Come find me in the shop. There are so many things you need to know, and we don't have much time. You need to make your decision quickly, I'm afraid. Lives depend on it."

"No pressure though, right?" I whimpered.

Callum issued me a cryptic smile before turning to walk back toward the crowd in the distance. About halfway down the alley, he stopped and turned back to face me. "You deserve to have a taste of the life you were meant to live," he called back. "You deserve good things, you know."

I raised my hand and said, "Thanks?" before doubling over, my hands on my knees, as I tried to stave off a wave of nausea.

When I looked up, Callum was gone.

GOODBYES

AFTER I'D RECOVERED MY CELLPHONE AND CHECKED TO MAKE SURE the bleeding from my wound had stopped, I stumbled out onto High Street. I still had my mask in my hand, but I was too afraid to put it on. My breathing had calmed a little, but I still felt like I was floating somewhere between reality and an impossible dream-world where nothing was quite as it seemed.

I couldn't get the image of the wolf's face or the huge wooden door out of my mind. I couldn't forget what I'd seen and heard, both from my abductor and from Callum.

As my eyes adjusted to the streetlights flickering overhead, I looked around until I spotted Will and Liv bouncing their way through the thinning crowd toward me.

"Vega! Are you okay?" Will asked, pulling his mask off. "Where the hell have you been?"

"I…I was just catching my breath," I replied.

"You're as white as your mask," Liv added. "What happened to you?"

I opened my mouth to reply but slammed it shut again. Telling them the truth would be a mistake. At best, Will would have me committed to the nearest psychiatric ward.

And at worst…No. I didn't even want to think about it.

"I lost track of you guys when a car pulled out in front of me," I finally stammered. That part wasn't a lie, after all. "The guy nearly clipped my leg. I jumped back and hit my head on the corner of that building back there." I held out the wad of napkins Callum had given me, still red and wet with my blood.

"Oh my God," Liv gasped. "Are you all right?"

"I'm fine," I assured her. "I looked for you, but I guess I lost you in the crowd. I never realized how many tall people there are in Fairhaven."

"Well, don't lose us again," Will said as he leaned over to inspect the back of my head. "You had us worried." I could tell he suspected I was hiding something, but he didn't press me.

"Don't worry," I said, relieved beyond words to have my brother and my best friend by my side. "There's no place I'd rather be right now than with the two of you."

Stopping along the way to buy three cups of iced tea from one of the many vendors lined up along the parade route, we managed to finish the procession without incident. I didn't see Callum again, or the strange ferret-girl and scar-boy. At one point I reached for the key around my neck, feeling its jagged outline through my shirt. Without understanding why, I knew the trinket was more important and powerful than anything I'd ever come across. It had nearly gotten me killed, but it had also saved my life.

As for Callum's talk about magic doors and mysterious academies…on the one hand, it was an insanity overload. On the other hand, stranger things had happened.

I just couldn't think of any at the moment.

After walking Liv to her house, Will and I headed home and plopped down on the couch to immerse ourselves in a sci-fi movie marathon, a tradition we'd begun years earlier with our father. The goal was to stay awake as long as possible—all night, if we could manage it—until finally passing out in a pile of couch cushions and popcorn bits.

None of the films we watched was especially good, so we wound up talking through most of them. I asked Will about the engineering courses he would be taking in September at the University of California. He answered to the best of his abilities, then, cleverly changing the subject, he asked me about school, boys, and dating.

"Anyone in your life?" he asked point blank after tip-toeing around the topic for a little.

"Sort of," I blushed before realizing what I was saying. "I mean no. I mean, there's no one in particular. You know me. I don't hang out with anyone but you and Liv."

He nodded and gave me an "I don't believe you" glance out of the corner of his eye, but he didn't press me on it.

Right on cue, I found myself thinking about Callum. About how he'd found me in the alley and how he'd scared off the psychotic man who'd come after me. His threats, the anger in his fierce eyes, the power behind his words. I couldn't wait to see him again, to get some answers to the questions I'd been too afraid to ask. All of a sudden, I desperately wanted to set my eyes on him again, if only to prove to myself he was real. I couldn't get his face or his voice out of my head, but now that I was no longer under threat, they felt like a dream, somehow.

After another three or four hours of bad movies and good conversation, Will and I got tired and agreed we'd both rather wake up in our beds than on the couch and loveseat. I gave him a hug goodnight and padded off to my room, where I collapsed onto my bed and fell into a restless sleep where dreams and reality wrestled all night for dominance.

The next morning, I woke up wiped out and bleary-eyed. I stumbled downstairs to find Will sitting at the kitchen island with two steaming mugs of coffee in front of him. He slid one of the mugs toward me as I dropped down with a grunt onto the stool across from him.

"Thanks," I grumbled, taking a tentative sip of the scalding hot drink. Normally I wasn't a big fan of coffee, but the morning air felt oddly frigid, especially for the middle of summer. I had to admit that I appreciated anything that might warm and wake me up all at once.

"How about some breakfast to wash that down?" Will asked, watching me with an amused grin.

"I'm not hungry," I said, my head in my hands. "Why do I feel like I've been hit by a car?"

"Probably because you almost were," Will reminded me.

I sat up, remembering the white lie I'd told Will and Liv the night before. "Right. The car."

"Sounds like you had a close call in that alley."

"You have no idea," I muttered into my coffee.

"Listen," Will said, standing and stuffing some snacks from the kitchen counter into a red backpack. "I need to know you're going to be okay here on your own."

"I'm legally emancipated," I reminded him. "I can look after myself. You know that."

"That's not what I mean. I know you can take care of yourself. You've been doing it practically since Mom and Dad died."

"Then what—?"

"I just worry about you, Vega. It's not a big house, but you're going to be alone in it. School is still a month away. Liv is leaving today, and I'll be gone. Even the bratty kids you sometimes babysit across the street are away at camp."

"And I'll be fine," I said, laughing. "I do best when left to my own devices. When's your flight, anyhow?"

Will whipped out his phone, his eyes going wide when he saw the time. "Jeez. Three hours. We'd better get going."

My heart sank. I knew his stay was really just a layover, but knowing I was losing him quite so soon was a shock.

"But you just got here!" I protested, jumping to my feet.

"I know. I'm really sorry. But hey—at least I got a chance to stop in for a day and spend some time with the most important thing in my life."

"Aw."

"By that, of course, I mean Liv's rubber zebra head."

"Jerk." I punched him, and he winced like he'd been slugged by a prize-fighter before throwing his arms around me and pulling me into a giant bear hug. Ten minutes later, after downing a piece of toast to go along with my morning coffee, I joined him outside, where he was tossing his bags into the trunk of his 2003 Toyota Matrix.

"She's seen better days," he said, running his hand along the strip of rust above the driver's-side door.

"Don't worry. I'll take good care of it—her—while you're gone."

"You should. She's yours now."

"Wait," I said, my jaw dropping. "You're giving your car to me?"

Will nodded. "There's no way it would make it out to California, but there's no reason you can't boot around town in it. This car served Mom well. It served me well. And now it's your turn. Call it a slightly-late, extremely crappy birthday present."

"Thanks, Will," I gushed. "I really don't know what to say."

"Don't get too excited," he said, patting the hood with his hand. "I'm already thinking what to get you when you turn eighteen, because I don't think this old beater is going to make it to your next birthday. Let's keep our fingers crossed that it makes it to next week."

"I'll get a job and pay for gas and stuff," I vowed. "I'll—"

But Will shook his head. "Don't even think about it. Mom and

Dad would have hated it if you did anything to distract you from school."

"But..."

"No 'buts.' We both know perfectly well what our parents would have wanted, and it wasn't for their seventeen-year-old daughter to find herself struggling to juggle work and school. Maybe go out and find yourself something more interesting than a part-time job to occupy yourself."

I got the distinct impression he was talking about boys, but I chose to ignore the suggestion.

"Okay, okay, I'll shut up now," he laughed. "Let's get going."

Out of habit, I started to get into the passenger side, but Will stopped me with a shake of his head. "Nuh-uh. You're in charge now. Time to take the wheel. Literally and figuratively."

I skipped over to the driver's side and slid in behind the steering wheel. The rush of being in control of something for once, plus the knowledge that my time with Will would soon come to an end, made the drive go by all too fast.

When we'd reached the airport, I pulled us up to the curb and slid the chugging Matrix into the long line of cars already idling as families and friends said their last goodbyes before sending their loved ones on their way. Suitcases and backpacks of every color sat on the concrete walkway outside the revolving doors to the terminal.

The place was a flood of hugs and smiles and tears, and there was a terrible impermanence to it all. Everyone on the move. Everyone leaving to go somewhere else. So much attention being paid to the ones about to catch a flight. But what about the rest of us—the ones being left behind? We needed hugs and good wishes more than anyone.

Will opened his door but didn't get out. "What's going through that mind of yours?"

"You're lucky," I said, staring straight ahead through the windshield at a burly man lugging suitcases out of the back of a taxi.

"You're lucky for all the things you're going to do out west. All the adventures you'll have. The things you'll learn. The people you'll meet."

"I *am* lucky. But not because of any of that. I'm lucky because, after all those people and adventures, I have you to come home to."

"You will come home, won't you?"

"Of course I will. How can you even ask that?"

I rested my head on the steering wheel and looked at my big brother, who smiled and reached over to pat my hair.

"I better get going."

"I know."

Will stepped out of the car, and I pushed my door open and ran around to join him on the curb. I flung my arms around his waist and held him tight, willing him to stay but knowing he couldn't.

As we said our last goodbyes, a sense of impending dread wormed its way through my mind. With Will's departure, I was losing my most loyal protector, the one person on earth who'd always seemed to understand me. But something told me that even Will wouldn't be able to protect me from whatever mayhem was in the process of being unleashed on my life.

"I have a layover in Dallas," he told me. "It'll be too late by the time I get to California to call tonight. But I'll be in touch soon, I promise."

I nodded miserably, unable to avoid remembering how empty the house felt without him for the month of July. August would feel even longer.

"I'll be back to visit in a couple months," he assured me. "I'll FaceChat you lots, too."

"Great," I replied. "I get to hang out in front of a computer camera. You know how much I love that."

"Stop it." Will took me by the shoulders and looked me in the eye. "Vega, you've always been so down on yourself. Let me give you some brotherly advice."

I cocked my head and stared at him, humoring him.

"Yes?" I asked.

"Know your worth," he said. "Know how great you are. Don't let the world tell you otherwise, because it *will* try. Be strong. Prove to everyone, but most of all to yourself, just how incredible you really are. Fight for what's right and for what's rightfully yours."

"Rightfully mine?" I asked. It was an odd thing to hear him say in light of everything that had happened yesterday.

"You know what I mean," he added. "You're talented. You're gifted. Everything comes easy to you if you just put your mind to it. I know you do well in school, but you always throw a wrench into your own social life. Don't be someone who sabotages herself on purpose to prove to the world that you don't deserve the best things. You should be proving how amazing you are, because that's the real you. And I think you know it."

"Hmm. This is strangely sincere talk from you, Big Brother."

"Yeah, well, I figure I won't be seeing you for a while, and this might be my last chance. You know, in case I get hit by a truck or something."

"I appreciate it. But don't get hit by a truck, okay?"

"I'll do my best not to. As for you, don't spend too much time at home."

"What are you talking about?"

"I know you. You'll hole yourself up for the rest of the summer with a stack of books, read until your eyeballs dry out, and never put yourself out there."

"Put myself out where?"

"You know. Into life. Take a chance. A leap of faith. All that hokey clichéd stuff."

"I promise. If a chance comes along, I'll leap. I'll probably break an ankle doing it, too."

"That's all I ask," Will laughed. He slung his backpack over his shoulder and threw me a smile that looked like it might turn quickly into a quivering frown.

"Don't you dare cry, or you'll get me started," I said, hugging him close and burying my face in his shoulder. "I'll miss you, Will. And thanks. For everything."

As I watched my brother walk toward the sliding doors and into the terminal, I forced down the sob forming in my throat.

Will spun around one last time and called out, "Love you, Vega!"

"Love you, Will," I mouthed through a smile as the tears streamed down my cheeks.

I hopped into the car—*my* car—wiped my eyes, gave my head a good shake, and drove back to town, where I was determined to track down and get some actual answers from one Mr. Callum Drake.

Maybe it was time to take that leap of faith.

THE ENEMY

AFTER TUCKING THE CAR INTO OUR DRIVEWAY, I SHOWERED, THREW on some clean clothes and began the short walk to High Street and the Novel Hovel. I supposed driving was an option, but I'd always enjoyed wandering around town on foot too much to become reliant on a rusty old car—besides which, walking would give me time to figure out what I planned to say to Callum.

I turned onto High Street, my pulse quickening as I approached the bookstore. By the time I was a block away, I was already imagining how foolish I'd sound when I started asking questions. I began to wonder again if the whole thing might have been some extended hallucination. Callum would probably look at me like I was completely insane when I brought up the wolf-man from last night, or the girl whose ferret doubled as a large predatory cat.

Or, worse still, he'd look at me like what I was saying made perfect sense.

I wasn't sure which potential reaction freaked me out more.

I'd just started to pick up my pace when I realized something in the air was changing, and quickly.

The comforting hum of air conditioners in shop windows

died. No cars whizzed by. I suddenly found myself surrounded by oppressive, impossible silence. The only thing that showed any sign of life was me.

The world had come to a stop…just as it had the previous day.

I froze, my throat parched with fear. When the world had gone still yesterday, Charlie had handed me the dragon key that had set a whole chain reaction of mayhem in motion. I wasn't sure I could take any more chaos just now.

I stared ahead toward Perks, but this time, there was no sign of Charlie or Rufus. No sign of any life, in fact. Downtown Fairhaven was a ghost town.

Hesitant, I began to walk again, hoping it was a fluke. Maybe a power outage had caused the abrupt silence. I'd heard that such things happened when too many people were using air conditioners and televisions at once. I told myself to keep walking, to get away from High Street, which seemed to be ground zero for mayhem. But before I could make it more than a few steps, the sound of a long, low snarl erupted from behind me.

No, no, no. Please, no.

I slammed my eyes shut, freezing in place as my hands clenched into tight fists. *Please,* I murmured again inside my head. *Make it stop. Make it go away.*

But the growl came again, accompanied by a string of several more, as if the sounds were multiplying behind me.

I spun around to see a massive white wolf standing in the middle of High Street, its bright eyes locked on my own. Coming at me from the direction of the Commons was another wolf, this one gray, with black streaks in its fur. Then another, and another, until four of them stood—two on the street, the other two on the sidewalk—in a menacing semi-circle in front of me. I stepped away, my back pressed to the brick façade of a single-story building housing a bank, a sandwich shop, and one of the local real estate agencies.

Cornered, I stared at the enormous animals, my hands shaking. I started to cry. Not out of fear, though. This was pure, unadulterated anger. Anger at being faced with death for the second time in twenty-four hours. Anger at being the apparent target of some army of supernatural beings with nothing better to do than terrorize me.

The wolves growled, the hackles on the backs of their necks quivering in a bristling fury. Although they looked like giant mutant dogs, there was something else about them that horrified me.

Something beyond animal. There was an intelligence in their eyes, along with a palpable anger and hatred.

Just like I'd seen the previous evening on the face of the man in the alley.

Waerg.

That was it. That's what Callum had called the strange contorted man-wolf who'd thrown me against the wall. The man who'd almost killed me.

And now there were four of them.

They approached with small steps, heads low as growls erupted from deep in their broad chests. Their paws looked heavy enough to press their imprints right into the concrete sidewalk.

As I stared in disbelief, a strange, feminine voice began to speak inside my mind. *You have something that we need, Vega Sloane. Give it to us, and we'll leave you in peace.*

An eerie calm swept over my mind. Like a person possessed, I pulled the key out from under my hoodie and held it up to the growling beasts. "Is this what you want?" I asked. "You can have it. It's all yours."

I was shocked to hear my own words.

They were definitely coming from my mouth, but I wasn't in control of them. They made no sense, for one thing. Last night I'd realized the key was of vital importance. Callum had threatened to kill someone to protect it and me.

So why was I now offering it freely?

Before I had a chance to toss the key at the advancing pack, the light, distant sound of chiming bells caught my attention. I looked down the sidewalk past the wolves to see Callum stepping out of the bookstore. Without a second's hesitation and with his face in a rage, he sprinted in my direction, looking like he might attack all four wolves at once. But he came to an abrupt stop after only a few seconds, like something had halted him in his tracks—some invisible barrier that was now keeping him from coming any closer.

He shouted, but my mind had clouded over, and I couldn't make out what he was saying. He pounded with his fists against what looked like nothing but the air in front of him. The way his fists bounced off, it must have been a barrier as hard as steel.

The wolves turned to peer at Callum over their shoulders before twisting back to face me.

He can't help you, the soothing female voice spoke to my mind. I looked from one wolf to the other until my eyes settled on those of the white beast. Its eyes were blue, intense, and eerily familiar. I'd stared into them once before.

Then, just like now, fear had overcome me.

"What are you doing to him?" I asked, my gut churning with terror as I pushed away the fog that had overtaken my mind. *She's manipulating me,* I thought. *She's putting ideas in my head—trying to soothe me so I'll be compliant.* I shook my head hard, trying to free myself of her mental grip.

I'm keeping him from interfering in our affairs, the voice said. *This can be a simple exchange: We get the key. You get your life. Callum Drake will be safe.*

I answered her with a silent stare, a feeling of strength rising up inside me as I narrowed my eyes.

No, I thought. *I can't give the key up. It's too important. I may not understand why, but if I give it to them, everything will be destroyed. The only thing I know is that I have to protect it, no matter what.*

The female voice practically sang in my head then, a soothing, melodious tone that made me all but forget why I cared about the key in the first place. *Come, now. You can live a life unsullied by the scourge of the Old Magic. You can return to normalcy. Isn't that what you want most? Peace and quiet, here in this lovely little town of yours? Don't you want to forget everything that's happened?*

"Yes, it's what I want," I began, once again overtaken by her charms. "All I want is to go back to how things were."

How things were, the voice said. *Yes, of course. Before your parents were taken from you...*

With those words, the feeling of calm that had settled into my bones shattered, and my jaw clenched. "Don't talk about my parents," I snapped. "And don't pretend to know what my life was like before they died."

Apologies, the voice said. *It was not my intention to offend. Give us the key freely, and we will leave in peace.*

I had to admit I was tempted by her words. Angry though I was, I looked down to see my hand reaching out to offer the key to the white wolf. I could feel her inside my head, probing around, trying to find the most vulnerable part of me, to find a crack in my mental armor. Yet some part of me *wanted* her there. I wanted her to take away this curse, this trinket that had haunted me ever since Charlie had handed it to me. The thought of being free of it made me feel light, free as a bird...

I took a step forward, holding the key out with tremulous fingers, ready to hand it over, when a voice cried out.

"Vega! Stop!"

I looked up to see Callum, still trapped behind the invisible barrier separating him from me and the wolves. His face was strained as he struggled forward, like he was pushing a massive wall, inch by inch, with every ounce of his strength.

"But they want it," I said evenly, all emotion stripped away. "I think they should have it—don't you?"

Even as I heard myself say the words, I began to realize they didn't come from a place inside me. It was this wolf, this Waerg—she was slipping the thoughts and words into my head, somehow. She was controlling me. I felt like I'd been taken out of my body and was watching from a distance as someone manipulated me like a helpless cloth puppet.

"The key was given to you for a reason," Callum yelled. "Use it! You know what to do, Vega! Go through the door. Accept your fate!"

The sound of his voice jarred me back inside myself. I recalled the door that had sprung up in the alley—broad, tall, with a carved dragon decorating its surface. The *Breach,* Callum had called it.

Glaring at the white wolf, I ripped the key from its chain and shut my eyes, trying to conjure the door. I had no idea how to do it, but still, I tried. In my mind I painted every inch of the door, from top to bottom, until I could all but feel it.

I opened my eyes to see it hovering in the air before me, but this time it didn't seem solid as it had last night. Now it was nothing more than a nebulous hologram, flickering and fading in and out like a waning light. Beyond its surface I could see the faces of the wolves, lips drawn back in angry snarls.

The white wolf stepped forward, and as one paw moved in front of the other, her shape altered. After a second, the woman I'd seen in the park the previous day stood before me, the same silvery-white hair and dark red lipstick framing her face.

My breath caught in my throat as I stared at her, hatred bubbling up inside my chest.

"It's all right, Vega," she cooed. "You have nothing to fear from me. I'm here to help you get back to your old life. I'm here to take away the fear you've been feeling, you poor dear."

As much as I fought them, the words began to sooth me once again. Just as the woman had promised, my fear dissipated, only to be replaced with a blanketing sense of calm. I felt a smile trace its way over my lips as I took a step toward her, holding my hand out once again in offering.

"No!" Callum cried out. "She's in your head. She'll destroy you if you let her stay there!"

He was right. I could feel the woman rifling through my mind like she was leafing through a filing cabinet. Yet I couldn't find the energy or the will to care, somehow. I found myself welcoming her like an old friend who comes in for a glass of iced tea. *Please, be my guest.*

Iced tea, I thought with a wistful smile. My Nana used to serve me and Will iced tea when we'd go to visit.

Nana, who had written me that birthday card and given me the supposedly unbreakable chain I wore around my neck now. What was it that she'd written in that card?

...the end of an old life and the beginning of a new one...challenges and danger ahead...this silver chain will save your life...

I drew my eyes to the key I was holding. When I saw how close I was to handing it over, I jerked my arm backwards.

"No!" I shouted. I shut my mind off, closing down my emotions as I'd done so many things over the years since my parents had died. Damn it, if there was one thing I was good at, it was pushing people away. "Get out of my head!" I snarled, locking eyes with the woman. "I know what you're doing to me, and it's not going to work."

An awful, unnatural grin twisted the woman's thin lips. She narrowed her eyes, staring at me with a malevolence unlike anything I'd ever seen or felt in my life.

"You miss your parents, don't you?" she asked. "Every day you miss them. Every day, you wonder if you could have prevented their deaths. Of course the truth is, it's all your fault."

I shook my head and slammed my mouth shut, grinding my teeth before growling, "I told you not to talk about my parents."

"You were meant to be with them, you know," she said, twisting her hand around to examine a set of bright crimson nails. "You were meant to die that night four years ago, along with them. It's a pity you didn't—then you wouldn't have to deal with all of this. But to know now that they died because of you…they died because you were the target. I can only imagine how you must feel."

Nausea swept through me as I stared, horrified, the grim recollection of that awful night churning through my mind like rapids in a river.

I was thirteen when my parents died.

Will was graduating from high school that afternoon, and I was meant to attend the ceremony with my parents, but I was recovering from a bout of food poisoning. My mother had offered to stay home with me, but I'd assured her I was all right and that they should go without me.

After the ceremony, Will had expressed an interest in hanging out with his friends, so, after calling to make sure I was all right, my parents drove to their favorite restaurant at an inn outside of town. It was situated off a twisting country road flanked by thick woods.

A witness, a bartender driving in the opposite direction on his way to work, told us how something—a large animal that looked like a wolf—had run out in front of my parents' car. My father had swerved to avoid it, sending the car flying off the road. It had flipped three times as it careened down a steep embankment before colliding with a deep-rooted tree. According to the first-responders and the doctor who met with me and Will at the hospital, our parents had died instantly.

The wolf, I thought, *the one that caused the accident…was it true? Could it really have been one of these creatures?*

I dropped to my knees, just like I'd done four years ago in the hospital, sorrow overtaking me so that I couldn't so much as straighten my spine.

"Give me the key," the woman snarled.

"No," I said, my head low. "I won't."

"Give it to me, and I'll make the memory fade," the woman said. "Give me the key, and I promise you, I'll take your pain away, once and for all."

The offer was all too tempting. Every day since my parents had passed away, I'd wanted something to heal me, to take away the hole that had formed inside me like a bottomless pit. But even if this woman was telling the truth—even if she could help me, would she extend the same kindness to Will? To my Nana? Would she take away their pain and grief?

No. Of course she wouldn't.

I drew my head up and looked past her to Callum, who had stopped fighting whatever power was keeping him from me. The determined expression on his face had altered to one of pain. By some inexplicable twist, I knew he was suffering the loss I was reliving, like it was happening all over again—this time, to him.

I'd always despised the way people had looked at me since Will and I lost our parents, like I was a broken girl who could never be mended. I would have preferred they stare at me with malice and disdain, because at least I could hate them for it. Sympathy was cruel. It was a blanket I could never quite shrug off, but one I also could never quite accept. Being pitied made me feel weak, useless, like the world's expectations of me had dwindled to nothing. But the way Callum was looking at me was more than mere sympathy or pity. It was a look of pure understanding, with a shared sorrow that told me he knew loss as acutely as I did.

As I stared at him, though, Callum's expression changed. His brows met, his lips curved down into a fierce grimace. "You know what you need to do," he cried out through the invisible barrier, his voice low and resonant. "They won't stop at the key, Vega. They're going to kill you whether you give it to them or not. If they have to, they'll destroy the key along with you!"

I stared at my fist, which was clenching the key so tightly now that its sharp edges were digging into my flesh.

Callum was right. I knew what I needed to do.

I only hoped I could find a way to do it.

"The key," the woman snarled again, taking a step forward.

I shook my head, and without a word, without entirely knowing why I was doing it, I waved a hand through the air. The wispy hologram of a door that had been hovering weakly turned massively solid, an imposing structure springing to life in the middle of the sidewalk. Determined, I jammed the dragon key into the glowing keyhole and twisted it until I heard a click.

I didn't know what awaited me on the other side. But whatever it was, I had no choice but to face it.

PART II
THE OTHERWHERE

SEEKER'S WORLD

ROLLING GREEN HILLS SURROUNDED ME ON ALL SIDES. A WARM breeze lapped at the long grass coating the gentle slopes in a series of slowly ebbing waves. The air in this place, whatever this place *was*, was more invigorating, more pure, than anything I'd ever inhaled in my life. I felt as though I'd walked into a young, unsullied world that had never so much as heard of internal combustion engines or pollution-emitting factories.

As I looked around, I could feel my lungs filtering out every chemical they'd ever taken in. I breathed deep, and a feeling of calm settled over me. The torment I'd felt a moment ago was gone—at least temporarily—only to be replaced with a quietly pulsing sense of euphoria, as if a potent drug had been injected directly into my veins.

It wasn't the worst feeling the world.

But it might have been the strangest.

"Where am I?" I asked out loud. On a whim I pulled my cell phone out of my bag and clicked the side button to light up the screen. Maybe there was a tower around here somewhere. If I could just get a signal, maybe my GPS could tell me where I'd ended up.

But when I looked down at the screen, I saw that the usual background photo of Will and me on our living room couch had disappeared. In its place was the image of a long silver sword against a white background. The usual date and time stamps were gone, and no bars showed to indicate whether I had any sort of connection to the outside world.

"Okay," I said out loud, still fully aware that talking to myself was hardly the way to prove my sanity. "This is…different."

Staring at the sword, I got overwhelmed with a sense of déjà vu. I was about to dismiss the feeling when it occurred to me: this wasn't the first time I'd seen that image. It had been on the cover of the book Callum gave me on my birthday, the book I'd left behind when the woman in the park accosted me.

I tapped the picture with my index finger, and a title page appeared. My phone, it seemed, had morphed into an electronic version of Callum's book. I dragged my finger across the screen, hoping and fully expecting to see at least a few familiar icons. But nothing. Everything on my phone was gone.

Everything but this book.

Seeker's World
An Invitation to the
Academy for the Blood-Born.

I tapped on the title and flipped through a few pages until I came to a table of contents. The first chapter listed was called "The Academy." I clicked the word and my screen brought me to a page that read:

The Academy is an ancient, fortified structure of white stone, set on the edge of a sprawling cliff, a wall of solid rock that drops down to the sea far below, where brutal waves crash against the shore.

On the other side, dense woods rise up to greet the base of the castle's fortifications. There is no road in. Only the few who are invited may enter, and all those who choose to attend must find their way there by some means or other, as an ancient magic protects the Academy's walls.

The invited are known as the Blood-Born.

If you are reading this, you are one of the invited.

Blood-born. Callum had mentioned that word. According to the screen, I was one of them. That should have freaked me out, but instead, it gave me a strange sense of calm, of purpose, like I had a real role in the world for once in my life.

Of course, this wasn't exactly the world where I'd hoped to have a role.

Okay, Vega. Let's take stock: You're here. This is not a dream. No one's slipped you any hallucinogenic mushrooms. That you know of. That leaves...what?

I spun around to look for any sign of the fortress-like structure the book mentioned. Maybe I was already being tested; maybe the Academy was standing right in front of me, hidden from view by some wild magic.

Or maybe I had to say a secret password to conjure it. *Academy Appearus,* or something.

"No," I muttered. "That's stupid. Then again, it's also pretty stupid that I'm standing in the middle of nowhere talking to myself, isn't it? Yes, Vega. It really is."

I was at the highest point of a broad, flat-topped hill, the grass soft and welcoming under my feet. To one direction in the far distance I could barely make out smoke rising from the chimneys of a series of small, thatch-roofed houses in an idyllic village nestled between two sloping hills. It was the only sign of life for miles.

It took me a moment to realize the door I'd stepped through had vanished, and somehow the dragon key had found its way back onto my silver chain. I was trapped in this place, at least for now—yet I didn't feel frightened.

For once.

I contemplated hiking toward the distant village, but it felt like a bad idea, as if intruding on their lovely little town would disturb the balance of this perfect, quiet land. Still, I couldn't help but think there must have been a reason the door I'd conjured had opened out into what seemed like the middle of nowhere. Or had I somehow messed up the summoning and leapt through the wrong door entirely?

My mind had been so addled by everything that had happened on Fairhaven's High Street that it wouldn't have surprised me to discover I'd screwed up royally and trapped myself in some sort of no man's land. Count on me to have the power to conjure a door to nowhere while escaping giant mind-bending Waergs.

Oh, God. The Waergs.

My thoughts shifted suddenly to Callum. To how I'd left him alone with those awful, vindictive shape-shifting creatures, trapped as he was by some cruel magic. I had no idea what they planned to do to him, but I couldn't imagine it would be good. He told me in the alley that a single Waerg wasn't enough to take him down, but I couldn't imagine him fighting four of them off, especially when one of them was some kind of psychotic mind-controller. I hated the thought that Callum might be hurt for my sake, or worse. He risked his life for the second time to help me…

And I ran away and left him behind.

"He's okay," I told myself. "He has to be." Something told me he was stronger than he'd ever let on, that there was far more to him than a handsome face and a brilliant mind. Callum was somehow connected to this mysterious Academy, which meant he was probably more powerful than I imagined.

I stared out toward the horizon, trying to convince myself not to worry, and to my surprise, it seemed to work. All the tension, fear, and anxiety in my body washed themselves away as if whisked off by a warm wind.

Maybe this place really was magical after all.

"Pretty, isn't it?" asked a deep, rich voice that startled me out of my blissful trance.

I spun around to locate the voice's source, which turned out to be a tall man with gray hair, chiseled cheekbones, a prominent nose, and a series of dignified wrinkles that looked like a road map of his entire life story. His posture reminded me a little of a vulture, the way his shoulders hunched slightly and his chin jutted out over his chest. His long, unkempt eyebrows shaded gray-green eyes and strengthened the comparison.

He was dressed in what looked like an odd hybrid of medieval and modern clothing: a pair of scuffed, brown leather combat boots, combined with linen trousers and a loose-fitting tunic of white cotton. Over that, he wore a leather jacket that looked like something I might have found at a local men's shop in Fairhaven. It would have been an odd ensemble on anyone, but it was particularly odd on someone who looked like he could be anywhere from his late-fifties to two-hundred years old. The stranger reminded me a little of Mr. Collins, the history teacher at our school who was so ancient and of such an indeterminate age that Liv had once gruesomely suggested we "saw him in half and count the rings."

The only difference was that Mr. Collins was an absolute terror who freaked out at unsuspecting teenagers for sport. This man felt like the opposite. He felt familiar, somehow. Something about him—perhaps his hard, vaguely off-putting edge—appealed to me.

"Where are we?" I asked.

"You expected something else when you came through the dragon's door?"

As he spoke, I realized it was partly his voice that made me feel so comfortable. Like Callum's, it was soothing and lilting. His accent contained hints of England, but something else, as well—something vaguely exotic I couldn't quite place, as though it originated from a country I'd never heard of.

"I guess I did expect something else," I replied. "The description in the book…" I stopped myself before I could finish. For all I knew, he was an enemy, here to gather secrets about the Academy. "Actually, I don't know what I expected. For all I knew, I'd be walking into a cave, only to get burned alive by a giant dragon."

"Well, you're in the right place, Vega Sloane," the man said with a warm smile. "This is what's known as the Otherwhere, though it has other names as well. The part you see before you is called Anara. My name is Merriwether, and I am the Headmaster at the Academy for the Blood-Born. I'm here to guide you, to show you what you will be competing to save when the Trials begin."

"Right, the Trials," I breathed. "Callum mentioned something about that."

"Ah yes, Mr. Drake," Merriwether said. "You've been wondering what's become of him, haven't you? Yes, I can see it in your eyes. You're worried about what the Waergs in Fairhaven might have done to him."

I nodded. "A little, yeah."

"He's very strong—a fact you're probably already aware of. He broke free of the spell that kept him from you. He'll be just fine."

I breathed a sigh of relief. "I'm glad," I said, stifling a smile. "I mean, I'd hate for someone to get hurt because of me."

"Of course." Merriwether shot me a knowing look before continuing. "I must apologize to you for how everything has occurred. The book Mr. Drake gave you was meant to be your invitation—"

"Yes," I said, holding up my cell phone. "He said something about that."

"But of course, things went a little sideways in your home town, and the invitation was lost for a time."

"I was starting to think the disasters were all just part of the regular process."

"Not at all," Merriwether said. "Most Candidates never have to contend with the threats you faced on your home turf. You should never have been targeted like that...but then, there's a reason you were."

"Oh? What reason is that? Was it something I said?"

Merriwether looked at me for a moment, ignoring my question. "The Trials are the reason everything since your seventeenth birthday has led you to this place. When you and I have finished our little tête-à-tête here in the Anara Hills, I will bring you to the Academy to begin your training. Unless, of course, you decide you don't wish to attend after all."

"I'm here, aren't I?" I asked. "What makes you think I wouldn't want to attend?"

"Because you summoned the door out of fear, and you came through it as a means of escape," he said. "It seems you weren't exactly aching to attend an Academy about which you know virtually nothing—and I can't exactly say I blame you."

I started to object, but I stopped myself. He was right. But how did he know so much about what I'd been feeling? "I do want to attend," I said sharply, recalling with a sudden clarity what the Waerg woman had told me about the night my parents had died. "I *need* to. I have to find those people and..."

"Find who, now?"

I looked up at Merriwether's eyes only to realize he already knew the answer to his own question. "They killed my parents," I said slowly, my voice betraying me by threatening to break. Saying the words out loud brought the reality of the situation to the forefront of my mind: My parents' deaths could have been avoided. I now had an enemy.

One I wanted to kill with my own hands.

"So you're telling me you came here because you want revenge," Merriwether said. "You want to do to them what they did to your family. You want to take lives as a means to even the playing field, is that it?" His voice was filled with pity, and a profound sense of shame began to infect me as I listened to his assessment.

"I just want answers," I said.

"Ah. You want to know what it is that inspired the enemy to commit murder," Merriwether said softly. "You want to know what sorts of creatures could do such a thing."

I nodded.

"Well, if you come with me, you'll find out soon enough. But I should warn you, the Academy has trained the Blood-Born for centuries, and we don't deal in revenge. If your sole motivation in attending is to draw blood, you will find you have no place between the walls of our institution. Focus too much on those who have died, and you will find it impossible to focus on the living…and it's the living who are important now."

"But…" I began, slamming my mouth shut when I saw the look on the Headmaster's face. He was right. Nothing I could say or do would bring my parents back or make the pain go away. "I do want to learn. I want to know why I was invited. I want to understand who—*what*—I am."

"Good. That's an important first step."

"Tell me, then," I said, pulling at the chain around my neck and holding Charlie's gift out from under my shirt. "Why did I get this on my birthday? Is it something every Seeker gets when they turn seventeen?"

"Ah, the dragon key," Merriwether said with a wistful smile. "Such a pretty thing. It wasn't easy to get it to you, you know."

"Wait—you were the one who set the whole thing up?" I asked, recalling my terror when I'd seen Charlie's and Rufus's glowing eyes on High Street. "But how…?"

He nodded, a sly smile crinkling the crow's feet surrounding his expressive eyes. "Guilty as charged. Though it took a lot out of me. Casting the Old Magic across worlds isn't easy, you know."

I stared in awe. "You're a wizard," I breathed. "You're some kind of freaking inter-dimensional Gandalf."

"I have no idea what a Gandalf is, but suffice it to say that I use the gifts of my bloodline, just as you did to get here." Merriwether sidled over to position himself next to me, gesturing broadly to the lands around us. "I'm sure you'd like to know why it is that you've been called to this place," he said. "A place that remains largely untouched, peaceful, quiet. Much like your little town of Fairhaven. For now, that is."

"For now?" I asked. "You're telling me this place and Fairhaven are going to change?"

"I'm telling you exactly that, yes. Unless the coming war is stopped in its tracks."

"War?" With the utterance of the word I found my fingers trembling. I'd stepped through a door into something so much bigger than I'd ever imagined, something momentous and terrifying. "War against the Waergs?"

"Yes and no. The Waergs are merely agents of the enemy," Merriwether explained. With another sweep of his hand, the landscape began to alter. Lush green grass turned brown, then black. The charming thatch-roofed cottages in the distance turned to ash and blew away, littering the sky with ominous, dark gray snowflakes. Even as I watched, the feeling of profound calm that had settled deep inside me turned first to sorrow, then abject terror. An apocalyptic scene was unfolding before me, and the horror of witnessing pure destruction swept its way through my blood.

Then the ash blew away, and the hills around us, too. In their place, the town of Fairhaven shimmered to life. High Street, with the Commons on one side, the row of friendly shops on the other. I puffed out a sharp exhalation, relieved to see a familiar, happy sight. But just as it had happened to the Otherwhere, Fairhaven began to burn, to crumble to dust before my eyes. Fires raged here and there, the ancient trees in the Commons stripped of their leaves and incinerated, turning to black, skeletal remains of their former selves before crumbling to the earth.

"Who would make this happen?" I asked, tasting foul ash on my tongue as I fought back tears. "And why?"

"The why is simple: Because she thrives on chaos," Merriwether said bitterly.

"And the who?"

"They call her the *Mistress*."

THE LIBRARY

THE MISTRESS.

The word sent a shiver trembling down the middle of my back. The last time I'd heard it was in the dark alley in Fairhaven, on the lips of the strange and terrible man who'd tried—and failed—to take the key from me last night.

"Who is she?" I asked. "Why would she want to destroy such a peaceful place?"

Merriwether swept his hand over the air once again, and the world around us altered for a third time. The ruins of Fairhaven disappeared, and green hills cropped up on all sides of us, a mesmerizing sight that allowed me to exhale a sigh of relief.

"Her servants call her the Mistress. But we call her the Usurper Queen," the Headmaster said. "She stole the throne in this place some time ago, though we've managed to keep her forces at bay for many years. But she's rising in power again. She's been building massive armies, capable of ravaging this land as well as your own. Which is why you—and others like you—have been summoned to the Academy to help us. We need one of your kind—a Seeker—to help us take her power from her."

"I'm sorry," I said, "I don't quite understand. Even if I was selected—even if I somehow won these Trials you've mentioned, how could I possibly help you to take her power?"

"Because it's a Seeker's fate," Merriwether replied. He tilted his head before adding, "But of course you don't understand. Why would you? This will require some explanation, and visual cues would be helpful. So please, close your eyes."

I stared at him, confused as to how I was supposed to receive visual cues if my eyes were sealed shut.

He let out an impatient sigh and said, "Just do it. Please. Trust me, Miss Sloane."

I wasn't exactly in the mood or the position to trust a total stranger. On the other hand, he seemed honest enough. Plus, he knew Callum. And, on top of that, if he really wanted to harm me, he could have done so in a million ways by now, all with my eyes wide open. So I did a quick mental calculation, figured my chances of being hacked to pieces by this guy were pretty low, and closed my eyes.

Just not all the way.

"No peeking,' he said, sounding slightly annoyed. "It won't work unless you're fully accessing your mind's eye."

"Okay, fine," I sighed, clamping my eyes tight, my fists in a ball just in case I needed to throw a couple of punches in self-defense.

With my eyes properly sealed, Merriwether continued. "Picture the inside of a large, many-levelled library, open at its center, with wrought iron spiral staircases on either side. Got it?"

"Got it."

"The expansive room is capped with a vast stained-glass dome. Carved into a series of stone columns supporting its levels are fire-breathing dragons and sword-wielding warriors clad in armor, fighting armies of wolves and other beasts. Got it?"

"Yes."

"When you walk into the space, you smell leather and oak, and a feeling of familiarity permeates your mind…despite the fact you're quite sure you've never seen anything like this before. Got it?"

"Leather and oak. Got it."

As I answered him, an image unfolded in my mind as though I was opening up a large map, each square foot springing to life as I directed my gaze around the space. But even as I looked at one section, another would disappear.

"I'm picturing it, I think," I said. "But I'm not sure I've got it right. It feels...incomplete. Like I can only see it in bits and pieces."

"Open yourself to the *idea* of the library," Merriwether said softly, his voice floating its way into my ears. "Invite the place into your mind, rather than trying to create it from scratch. Feel its wholeness, its existence, in your blood. Images of scholars, hanging on the walls. Books bound in leather. Glowing lamps on long tables, lighting the place warmly for readers. *Feel* the place, rather than merely thinking of it. Know how real it is, and it will become real."

I did as he asked, trying desperately to open myself to the possibility I might conjure such a place from nothing.

It started out as an impossible task. Then an improbable one.

But after a few more seconds, it didn't seem quite so daunting anymore. In fact, the feeling of creation, the idea of me conjuring an entire environment from scratch felt kind of...right.

"I've got it," I said quietly after a time, scared to disturb the totality of what I'd created.

"Good, good," Merriwether said. "Now, bring us there."

I popped my eyes open, shattering the illusion like a crystal glass. "*Bring* us there?"

Merriwether nodded. "That's what I said, isn't it? You are a Seeker of the Blood-Born, after all, but you're not only that. You are a Summoner of Doors. Unless you don't think you have it in you to transport yourself all the way to the Academy..."

"Of course I have it in me!" I shot out defensively before clapping my mouth shut. Fortunately, the look on the old man's face told me he was amused by my determination rather than annoyed at my outburst.

"Sorry," I said. "I just need a moment to find it again."

I closed my eyes for the second time and pictured myself standing once again in the massive library. My mind filled with everything from the scent of wood polish to the detail in the stained-glass ceiling and its rainbow of scholars, dragons, knights…and something he hadn't mentioned: a large, gray castle-like structure, perched on the edge of a cliff.

"The library where we're going," I breathed, "it's inside the Academy?"

"Yes, it is."

A smile made its way across my lips. Merriwether might have been right—maybe when I'd first opened the dragon door and stepped through, it was with rage and revenge on my mind. But now all I wanted was to find the place where there were others like me. A place where the entire purpose of being was to make the world a better place. To fight against people like this one they called the Mistress.

When I opened my eyes again, a new door hovered in the air before me. This time it was crafted out of pure white wood, an open book carved elegantly into its face. I was certain I could see letters and words floating nebulously in the air above the book's pages, but each time I tried to focus on them, they disappeared into the ether like clouds of vapor on a cold day.

Without a word, I pulled the key from the chain around my neck and unlocked the door, pushing it open and passing through with Merriwether right behind me. When we were both inside, the door fizzled away behind us, leaving no evidence it had ever existed.

Just as the Headmaster had described, a vast room stretched out before me, with long, tall shelves leading in every direction, each of them covered from top to bottom in leather-bound tomes. On the main floor in the center of the space was a series of long tables, lit with what looked like magically hovering oil lamps. On either side of the enormous space, iron spiral staircases rose ten stories into the air with a landing at each level.

Fiery chandeliers bobbed weightless overhead, mid-way up the interior of the enormous chamber, lighting the place with an orange glow that brought to mind the fires my family used to enjoy in our living room in the winter. A sense of bliss filled me, and I inhaled the scent of the space. I'd always loved being surrounded by books, and this library was like a finely-crafted dream of my own making. I couldn't help wondering if it had been designed to calm nervous newcomers like me.

"As your powers increase, you'll find that you can move very quickly between destinations," Merriwether told me as he led me to the base of one of the spiral staircases and began to hike up. "Summoning will soon be second nature to you."

"Excuse me. You said my powers will increase?"

"Yes. Your abilities as a Seeker. You will continue to change in the days to come."

"Will I develop the power to not throw up?" I asked, my arms clamped around my stomach. "Because I think I might be about to lose my lunch."

Merriwether laughed like I'd told a knee-slapper, but I was totally serious. As I looked around and absorbed what I'd just done, I was beginning to grow dizzy from seeing so much with my eyes closed, not to mention freaked out about how real it felt. I supposed I was also feeling just a little bit of terror at the idea of being killed by the woman known as the Mistress.

But if I went back to Fairhaven, I could die of regret, which might be just as bad—if not worse.

"Don't worry," Merriwether said, stopping on the stairs to give me a reassuring pat to my shoulder before proceeding to climb. "You wouldn't be here if you weren't supposed to be."

"Can all Seekers do this thing?" I asked. "I mean, is calling up doors *the* special Seeker power or something?"

Merriwether stopped climbing again and turned my way. "No. They don't all have your gifts. Nor do you have all of theirs —though you may find one day soon that you have more gifts than most. Now come with me. I want to show you something."

I wanted to ask him what gifts he was talking about. What was it I could supposedly do, other than conjure doors to mysterious places in my mind?

As we continued to ascend the multitude of stairs, the chandeliers climbed with us, glowing beacons lighting our way. It was only when we'd gone up six or so levels that I realized we were alone in the library. Not a soul was stirring, rifling through books, or sitting at the tables far below. For some reason, we had the place entirely to ourselves.

"You're wondering why no one is here," Merriwether told me as if in answer to the question I hadn't asked. "Why this place is empty, when it should be swarming with curious students."

"Sort of, yes," I replied. "I mean, if I had access to a place like this, I'd be here all the time."

Once again, though, the Headmaster declined to explain anything. Instead, he guided me the rest of the way up the curving stairway. When we'd finally reached the top level, he led me over to a glass display case stretching almost the entire length of the library. Inside was a lengthy piece of parchment, and on it was a long, straight line drawn in ink, with symbols at various points that seemed to denote moments in history.

"What are these?" I asked, pointing to what looked like a series of dates. They were marked with arrows and words like "Selection XXIV," "The Fall of the Dragon King," "The Usurping."

"Those are important points in the history of the Otherwhere," Merriwether replied. "The symbol that looks like a small circle marks an Opening."

"Opening? Of what?"

"Of the portals that join this world to yours. I told you that not all Seekers can do what you can—your gift enables you to move freely between our two realms. But others rely on the portals, which open every half-century or so. Unfortunately, the enemy also relies on them."

"What for?"

"Many, many years ago, when a man known as the Crimson King was in power, he cast a spell that opened a series of doors between our worlds. For a time, his forces moved into your lands. Armies that would conquer entire territories. Dragons, even."

"Dragons? But dragons aren't real. They're just in stories and movies and...oh, no. You're going to tell me they're real, aren't you?"

Merriwether raised an eyebrow. "The old stories—the ones that seem so far-fetched now—come from a time when dragons, allied with men, flew through your skies."

"Allied? But I thought..."

"You thought they flew around terrorizing humans," Merriwether said with a sigh.

"Well, yeah." I couldn't help recalling my dream in which a horrifying flying beast had opened its giant mouth to unleash hell on me. The creature didn't exactly scream *adorable puppy dog*.

"The truth is, for a time, the dragons and our people worked side by side toward a common cause. When they were in your lands, it was as protectors. Protectors of treasure, of armies."

"So what happened to them?"

"An enemy of the Crimson King began to threaten his reign. He had no choice but to bring his forces back to the Otherwhere...and that included the dragons, who fought in his army. Many of the beasts were killed, others enslaved, and the bond between dragon and human was severed."

"Are there still dragons? Here, I mean?" I asked, looking

around and half-expecting a giant fire-breathing lizard to melt a hole in the wall.

"There are," Merriwether said. "But you won't find them friendly. Most of them, anyway. There are, of course, some humans who can transform into dragon-kind, but that's something I'll leave you to learn about on your own time, as we don't have all day."

"Wait—hold on..." I gasped. "Did you just say there are men who can turn into—"

But Merriwether shot me a look that told me I'd be wise to stop asking questions.

"You have been wondering what's been happening to you since your birthday," the Headmaster said. "You're trying to sort out why strangers have been pursuing you, threatening you. Why the key you have in your possession is so very important."

I nodded.

"I mentioned the portals—the ones between our worlds. As I said, they open every half-century or so, thanks to a spell the Crimson King set in place long ago. In times of peace, it's not a bad thing. But now we have a tyrannical queen in power, and leaving the portals open makes both our worlds vulnerable to infiltration. There is only one way to seal them again, which brings me to you."

"Me?" I asked, my hands and legs trembling.

Merriwether nodded. "Every fifty years, the Seeker selected at the end of the Trials is given an important task: to locate the Relics of Power."

"And those are—?"

"Four objects scattered throughout your world and our own. They were hidden centuries ago, during the days of the dragons. They are the only things that enable us to seal the portals and protect the Academy."

"I don't get it. You said a Seeker looks for these objects every fifty years?"

"I did."

"But if a Seeker already found them, why search over and over again?"

"Because the objects fade, as does their power," Merriwether said. "Like melting ice, they each wane over time and finally disappear and find their way to a new hiding place. At that point, a new Seeker must be selected to find them, and the cycle begins again. It's our only way of keeping the peace and maintaining order."

I let out a long, slow breath. This was a lot to take in, and my brain was starting to hurt.

"Don't worry, Vega," Merriwether said. "Your only job at the moment is to decide if you wish to stay here, to train, to compete in the Trials. After that, we can worry about saving the world."

"I see. But you said there are other Seekers—other Candidates. I have to assume they'd be better than me at that particular job. I mean, you may find this hard to believe, but I have literally zero experience saving the world."

Merriwether let out a chuckle. "Yes. There are twelve other Candidates, each of whom has a powerful gift. I admit that they're a talented bunch, though it would be a pity to see you give in before you've so much as tried. You are, after all, one of the Blood-Born. You have it in you to be one of the best. Just like *she* was."

"She?" I asked, my curiosity piqued. "Are you talking about the Mistress again?"

"Hardly." Merriwether looked away, turning to a series of paintings on a distant wall stretching half the length of the library.

"Come," he said. "I'll show you."

He led me toward the row of portraits, some of which featured men in doublets, others displaying women in elegant gowns, until we reached one in particular. A young woman with blond hair and blue eyes, her mysterious smile reminiscent of the

Mona Lisa's. Something about her was oddly familiar, like I'd met her.

But where?

"Mariah Sloane," Merriwether said with a strange, distant smile. "This is, of course, your grandmother."

"Nana?" I asked, gawking at the painting. The young woman wore a dark green jacket and black pants and clutched a silver blade in her lap—a curved dagger of some sort. "My grandmother…was a Seeker?" I asked, baffled. *And from the looks of it, she was a badass.*

"Yes. Fifty years ago. Your grandmother faced many dangers and then some. She was the leader of the last cohort, and it was only because of her strength that we've managed to keep the Mistress at bay for so long."

I moved toward the portrait, marveling at how like my grandmother—and yet unlike her—the woman staring back at me was. Nana was small and, though she was energetic, she'd always given off an old-woman vibe that made it extremely difficult to contemplate her as some sort of fierce, bright-eyed, young warrior. Sure, she was a bundle of energy in her garden. And she could knit a sweater with her eyes closed. And no one made a better Shepherd's Pie. But this…?

"You really did have magical powers," I said softly to the painting. "All that time, Will and I were right." I spun back to look at Merriwether. "Did you know her?"

"I did," he said, his tone altering to something bittersweet.

"Have you seen her since she was here?"

He hesitated for a moment before replying, "Once, yes. A few years after she collected the Relics and turned them over to the powers that be. Your grandmother is a great woman. She sacrificed a good deal for both our worlds. She did everything she could to ensure that the Mistress—the Usurper Queen—would never come to her full strength."

I couldn't help but smile. So strange to think of Nana as a

young woman in her small Cornish hometown. A girl my age, confronted by the same strange series of events as I'd experienced. I wondered if she'd been as frightened as I'd been, or if somehow, she'd taken it all in stride. She was so confident, so knowledgeable.

Suddenly, I wanted to see her again, to get to know the woman I'd always thought I knew so well. I wanted to ask her about the silver chain she'd given me and how it had saved her life back in the day.

"So Nana—my grandmother—she competed in the Trials you're talking about? She...won?"

Merriwether nodded. "She did. Though I can't say she expected to. It can be overwhelming to walk into a situation such as yours. Some crumble when they realize the full significance of their task. She came close to giving up before the Trials even began, but in the end, she succeeded. Back then, the Mistress was only beginning to come into her power, of course. She'd just recently sent the rightful heir away from the capital and had begun to amass her forces."

"So, you're saying my Nana put a stop to that. She kept things from going too far."

"She brought us the Relics, yes. For a long time, we had all four in our possession. The only one that hasn't faded completely is the Orb of Kilarin."

Merriwether guided me over to another glass case concealed in a far corner of the library's top level. At first, it appeared to be empty. But as we approached, I could see that an object was floating inside it, flickering in and out of focus as I stared. It was a purplish orb, somewhat like a crystal ball, and hovering inside it was the image of a dark castle with tall, jagged towers. All told, the object looked like a grim snow globe bought from a gift shop in Hell.

"Its power is fading," Merriwether said, "and soon it, too, will vanish from this place. It has been under our protection for the last fifty years. The moment it disappears, the queen will send her minions to find it, just as she's already sent them to find the other Relics. Just as she sent them to find you, to acquire your key."

"What if I…I mean, what if the chosen Seeker fails to find the Relics first?"

"If the Usurper Queen obtains them all, then the Otherwhere will fall. The portals will open permanently, and the queen's agents will move through freely. Your world will be overtaken by those who move in shadow. Towns like Fairhaven will be overrun by Waergs and others, and the world will slowly burn."

"So, no big deal then," I muttered.

I stared at the orb, which flickered, disappeared, then seemed to flare to life again like a flame gasping for air. I eyed the strange structure lurking inside it, contemplating what would happen to an idyllic little town like Fairhaven if the creatures who'd haunted me since I'd turned seventeen took over. It was a tough and scary concept to get my head around, but when I thought about the strife and the suffering and the turmoil that already existed in my world—all of which I knew could easily one day make its way to Fairhaven—it didn't seem so outlandish or so improbable anymore.

For the first time, I knew without a doubt what I had to do.

"I want to compete in the Trials," I said, Will's advice echoing in my head. *Fight for what's right.* "I'll do my best—even if I'm not sure that'll be good enough. I want to help if I possibly can."

"Come, then," Merriwether said with a nod and an approving smile, leading me toward the nearest spiral staircase. "I believe it's time to introduce you to the Academy."

THE ACADEMY FOR THE BLOOD-BORN

When we reached a set of double doors at the base of the stairs, Merriwether stood to the side and gestured for me to proceed. But as I reached for the handle, both doors swung open without so much as the touch of my fingertips.

"Welcome to the Academy for the Blood-Born," Merriwether said in his rich, deep voice as a long hallway appeared before my eyes.

"The door?" I asked, my mouth open. "Did I do that?"

Merriwether answered me with a cryptic, "Hm."

Side by side, we walked into the hallway. Large, arched windows lined the walls on the right side, inviting beams of sunlight to splay out in big rectangles on the floor.

I wasn't much of a church-goer, but when I was little, I did like the way the millions of dust particles would dance in the light from the stained glass at the old church in Fairhaven. Oddly, there was none of that here. The air was as sterile as the glass was pristine. The light beamed in pure white.

Up ahead of us, uniformed students walked the hallway's length, stopping here and there to talk or to sit down on leather-upholstered benches to examine their books. Most of the kids were my age and were dressed in outfits that appeared to be a hybrid of school uniforms and some sort of medieval body armor. Red, navy blue, or fitted green leather waistcoats. Trousers that looked like Merriwether's loose linen pants, and boots that reminded me of the ones in all those war movies I'd watched with Will over the years.

The students' haircuts, too, were a mystery. Some of the boys looked like they'd just stepped out of 2019, their hair tidily trimmed, while others had shaggy, unkempt manes that brought to mind movies about Arthurian times. The girls generally had long hair, tied back in one way or another. I could only assume this was for practical purposes. Whatever sort of training they were undergoing at the Academy was probably physical, and I knew from years of experience with uncontrollable curls that there was nothing as distracting as locks of hair falling in your face while you were trying to focus on the task at hand.

A few of the students had weapons sheathed around their waists, while others looked as though they themselves *were* weapons. A boy who must have been at least seven feet tall slouched over a much smaller girl with a sheathed dagger tucked into a leather belt at her side. The girl had silver eyes, her pupils vertical like a cat's. The boy, meanwhile, had hands the size of frying pans, and looked like he could break through any one of the Academy's walls with little more than one angry punch.

"Who are they?" I asked Merriwether.

"The Academy's trainees. Soldiers in our army. The Academy has always been a training ground for the Gifted, even when we aren't at war. Someone needs to keep the peace, after all. Of course, most of the students you see right now are here to train as part of the Elite."

"The Elite?"

"The group who will accompany the chosen Seeker on his or

her task. It's a dangerous world, Vega. You've had a little taste of it already. But you should know we do everything here to ensure that the chosen Seeker survives to do their job."

"*Survives?* Isn't that a little extreme?"

Merriwether paused and grew stern, a deep crease forming between his eyes. He stopped me from walking forward with a firm hand on my shoulder. "This isn't a game. And it's not a fantasy or a dream. In your world, people talk in hyperbolic terms all the time. They say things like, 'I nearly died of embarrassment' when they trip in public or 'I'm going to kill you' when someone cuts them off in traffic. This isn't that. People here die doing what they must. Seekers die."

"That's reassuring," I muttered.

Merriwether shot me a look I couldn't quite decipher—he was either amused or annoyed by my sarcasm...or a little of both.

Any chance he had to figure me out was interrupted by the opening of a door at the far end of the hall. A familiar girl with skin the color of alabaster walked through, accompanied by a small orange tabby cat, who slinked along at her side with all the confidence of a Bengal tiger. The girl wore a dark blue leather waistcoat layered over a white tunic. I was beginning to realize the colors the students wore meant something—like they were some sort of classification system for the various groups.

"Niala!" Merriwether called out, gesturing to her. "Come here. There's someone I want you to meet."

The girl began walking toward us, her cat trotting at her heels like it had an invisible lead tied around its neck. As they approached, it transformed in front of my eyes into a large obsidian-black Husky. Its keen eyes remained locked on mine with the same appraising expression I'd seen on the ferret at Midsummer Fest, though now they were the lightest shade of blue.

"This lovely creature is Rourke, Niala's Familiar," Merriwether explained, gesturing to the dog but taking care not to touch him. "You've probably already figured out he's a shapeshifter." He said it as though he was simply explaining that the walls were made of stone. Like it wasn't something utterly mind-blowing. "Now, if you'll excuse me, I have a little business to attend to. Niala will show you around the Academy before the Assembly."

Merriwether walked away, and Niala turned to me.

"The Assembly is in the Great Hall," she explained as she began to walk down the long corridor. The dog padded along next to her, and I found myself doing the same. "You're the last Seeker Candidate to arrive," she added. "Which means it's time to start the Trials."

A knot of nervous excitement formed in my gut. "So soon?"

"Well, there will be some training first. I'm sure the Headmaster told you that."

"Right. Yes. Sort of. He told me so many things. I'm not sure I can keep them straight, to be honest."

"Listen," Niala said softly, looking at me out of the corner of her eyes. "I know this must be a lot to take in."

When I nodded but didn't say anything, she gestured around at the ornate hall, buzzing with its strange assortment of oddly-clothed teenagers, and dropped her voice to a more serious register. "I won't tell you not to worry or not to be afraid. Merriwether is a straight-shooter. I'm sure he told you what's at stake here."

I nodded again, still unable to get words past the lump in my throat.

"I'd offer you advice, but I don't have any. Everyone's experience here is different. Some can never get past the shock to the system of realizing they're living between two realms. Others get overwhelmed by the enormity of the task ahead or by the intensity of the training it takes to accomplish it. I will tell you this much: Don't forget why you're here or who you're doing this for.

Don't fight the pain or the fear you're going to experience. Instead, use it to guide and motivate you."

Finally, I swallowed hard and managed to squeak out a single question: "What did Merriwether mean about...people dying?"

Niala was quiet at first before telling me that Merriwether wasn't exaggerating. "And he wasn't trying to scare you," she added. "It's all part of the test."

"Test?"

"Of whether your fear of death is stronger than your love of life."

"Did I pass?"

Niala's indifferent shrug didn't inspire confidence, and I felt my heart race and my stomach drop.

After that, we walked in silence for a minute, my eyes moving from the buzzing students to the architecture to the view of ocean and cliffs outside. Uncomfortable and desperate to break the mortuary-like silence, I asked, "What exactly is a Familiar?"

"An animal companion who knows my mind." Niala stopped in her tracks and looked out a large window toward the distant horizon. For such an intimidating presence, it slightly confused me to register how gentle and soft her voice was. I pulled my eyes to her face, only to see that she wore the same expression as the dog at her side. Focused, intelligent, unreadable.

"I saw you in Fairhaven," I said. "On Friday evening. Talking to Callum. So that was Rourke? The ferret, I mean...and the panther?"

Niala laughed. "Yes, it was. He can shift into a variety of animals. A ferret. A bird. You name it."

"Well, whatever he was, thank you both for taking that man—Waerg—whatever he was—away."

Niala held up her hand. "I'm sorry for what you went through. The Waergs seem to have a great interest in you, though I'm not entirely sure why." She began walking again, leading me along the hallway toward a set of huge double-doors with Rourke loping along at her side. "They don't stalk every Candidate."

The heavy wooden double-doors swung open on golden hinges the size of my forearm.

"So how long am I…?"

"Are you going to be here?"

I nodded and blushed at the transparency of my anxiety.

"It's just…my brother will be trying to get in touch with me."

Niala let out another ringing laugh. There was something so easy about her when she smiled, so light, that I almost forgot how threatening she and her panther had looked in that alley. "No one will even know you're gone."

"Great. I'm so unimportant to the world that I won't be missed."

"It's not like that."

"Then what? Did they replace me with a clone?"

Niala grinned. "No."

"A robot look-alike? An alien pod?"

"I don't think so."

"Then what? Will's off at school, but he's still overprotective enough to freak out if he doesn't hear from me."

"During the Trials, time works a little differently. A day in the Otherwhere is next to nothing where you come from."

I must have looked confused because Niala stopped walking and swung around to face me. "Look at it this way. It'd take you about twenty-four hours to walk a hundred miles. You could probably cover the same distance in a car in about one hour. If you were a soundwave, you could do it in five seconds. If you were a beam of light, you'd travel a hundred miles nearly instantly. The point is, time runs between the realms in a slightly off-center parallel. In your world, you're you. Here, you're the beam of light."

"So Will is still…?"

"Where you left him."

"And Liv is still packing for her family trip?"

"If that's what she was doing when you came here, then yes. The Trials are in a week, our time. After that, and if all goes well, depending on what happens, you'll find yourself back in Fairhaven, almost like you never left."

"A *week*?" I all but shouted, glancing around self-consciously when I saw that a number of concerned faces had turned my way. I lowered my voice. "I'm supposed to learn everything there is about combat and being a Seeker and all that—in a week?"

"Don't worry. You'll have lots of help. Tell me, what's your gift?"

"My gift?"

"Your power. You know, what tricks can you pull out of your sleeve?"

"I...I can make doors appear," I said sheepishly. "Which seems pretty useless, now that I think about it."

"Not useless," Niala said. "It's a good start. You're a Summoner."

"Merriwether said something about that, but I'm not quite sure I understand what a Summoner is. I pictured myself leading rats out of Hamelin."

Niala let out another melodious laugh. She had a way of finding everything amusing without making me feel as though she was laughing at me, and I found myself appreciating her more with every passing second. Something about her was as reassuring and comforting as a security blanket.

She and Rourke reminded me a little of Charlie and Rufus. Constant companions who marched to their own beat and exuded a strange, quiet confidence. Neither seemed concerned for a moment that they were different, that they didn't necessarily fit smoothly into the world.

Then again, at the Blood-Born Academy, it seemed like no one—and yet everyone—fit in.

"A Summoner," Niala said. "Well, now, let's see. How do I

describe it? Your kind has the ability to conjure things. I've seen Summoners who can call forth solid fortifications with their minds. Some can call up weapons. Not permanent ones, mind you—but they last long enough to use against their opponents and make life fairly miserable for them."

"That actually sounds kind of fun," I said, picturing myself throwing a massive brick wall up in front of the next Waerg who came at me. The only problem was that I couldn't begin to imagine myself successfully casting such a spell.

Niala nodded. "I've even heard of Summoners who can call animals to their side to aid them in combat situations. Not like Rourke, though. I'm talking about wild animals. Hawks. Bears."

"What do they call someone with your gift?" I asked. "Having a Familiar, I mean."

I'm what they call a Tethered—it's the name they give to people with Familiars, because of our attachment. If something happened to Rourke or to me, we would wither and die. He's as much a part of me as my own heart."

"I see," I said, though I wasn't sure I'd ever felt that attached to anything or anyone in my life. It was a nice thought, though it frightened me, too. To be so dependent on another creature would mean utter trust and honesty between you. It would mean opening up and exposing one's inner feelings and vulnerabilities.

"There are also Sparkers here at the Academy," Niala added. "Skin-changers, Controllers, Diggers..."

"Diggers?"

"Mind-controllers. Manipulators. They get inside your head. They know what you're thinking or what you're planning before you do. They find ways to make you do the opposite."

That must have been what the Waerg woman on High Street was, the one who wormed her way into my mind.

"Sounds horrifying," I said, remembering all too well the feeling of knowing my thoughts and actions were no longer under my control.

"They can be horrifying," Niala agreed. "But if they're on your side, they can also be extremely helpful. Let's see, there are Summoners like you, of course," Niala added. "Oh, and I almost forgot about Jabbers."

"Jabbers?"

"Warriors. Powerful ones who are gifted with swords. You saw one in Fairhaven. The boy with the scar."

"Crow?" I asked, recalling what Callum had called him.

Niala nodded. "He's a Zerker—one of the students you'll see in the red gear. He's a bit rough around the edges..." She leaned in close and whispered, "but he's actually a teddy bear."

"You mean he transforms into a teddy bear?" I asked, my mouth open, my eyes wide with incredulity.

Niala really laughed that time. "A *figurative* teddy bear."

"That's too bad. I'd pay to see him morph into a red-shirted and pants-less Winnie the Pooh."

Her laugh was interrupted by the clanging of a bell somewhere in the distance. It was loud enough to make the Academy's entire foundations vibrate, and, out of instinct, I reached out and grabbed Niala's sleeve.

"Don't worry," she said, reaching out to take my arm in hers. "We need to get to the Great Hall, but we still have five minutes before the Assembly will begin."

Jogging along, she guided me down the long, bright corridor until we came to a left turn, which led us down another hallway. This one was lined with paintings, some of them of landscapes that looked a lot like the rolling hills I'd seen when I'd first entered the Otherwhere, others that depicted dragons in flight, fighting packs of massive wolves. Some of the dragons had riders wielding swords, while others fought on their own. Among the wolves were other large animals—bears, buffalo, even moose.

One painting was of a woman in a white dress who was holding a long sword, like the one on the Academy's banners. She was barefoot and standing at the edge of what looked like a pond.

"Who is she?" I asked.

"That's the Lady of the Lake," Niala said. "The original Seeker, they call her."

"The Lady of the Lake? As in the woman who gave King Arthur his sword?"

"Yep. Her name was Viviane."

I gasped, recalling that the woman in the park—the Waerg with the light hair—had called me *Daughter of Viviane*. I finally understood what she meant, though I wasn't remotely convinced that a woman called Viviane who handed swords to random young men had ever really existed.

In one painting there was a massive red dragon, seemingly confronting a knight. The dragon had a circle of spikes jutting out from the top of its head like a crown. I paused for a moment to stare at it. The creature was beautiful, its eyes a piercing shade of green-blue. It reminded me of something or someone I'd seen before, though I couldn't quite think who or what.

"The Crimson King," Niala said, stopping briefly. "He's the reason we're all here. The reason the Academy was founded."

"Is he riding the dragon?" I asked, squinting at the picture to see if I could make out a man on the creature's back.

Niala chuckled. "Not quite," she said. "He *is* the dragon."

"Wait—the King was a dragon?"

"Sometimes. He was a shape-shifter."

I stared at the painting, recalling what Merriwether had said in the library about humans who could transform into dragons.

"He was the most powerful magic-user and warrior anyone's ever known," Niala added. "He could transform into a dragon, but he also had something in common with you."

"What do you mean?"

"He was a Summoner," Niala said with a wink.

I stared at the painting again, mesmerized by the thought of someone so powerful. Someone who was an ally to the strongest beasts in the world.

I couldn't help but wonder, for about the millionth time, how I'd ever ended up in a place like this, or if I even deserved to be here.

THE GREAT HALL

THE GREAT HALL WAS APPROPRIATELY NAMED.

The cathedral-like room was a majestic, cavernous space with a ceiling high enough to give me a sore neck and a flash of dizziness just looking up at it. Towering stained-glass windows ornamented the walls to either side, depicting battle scenes, images of rolling fields, mountains, lakes, and other pretty scenery.

It reminded me of the high school gym back home—minus the basketball nets, the encased ceiling fans, and the musty reek of grunting boys pawing and bounding all over each other.

There was an air of dignity to this place that Plymouth High had never had.

There must have been two hundred teenagers, all grouped by the color of their uniforms, seated in the dozens of rows of wooden chairs. The students in blue sat in rows toward the front of the Hall, with those in green in the middle, and the ones in red at the back.

"The Zerkers like sitting as far away from the Headmaster as possible," Niala told me, "so they can get away with their crap."

"This place looks like a congregation of Skittles," I said.

Niala gave a little laugh and nodded her agreement. "I remember those from my last visit," she said.

My eyes skimmed over the students in crimson, noting their slouchy and undisciplined postures. They were a chatty bunch, not to mention aggressive. As I watched, one of the boys in the back row smacked the smaller boy next to him, which started a chain reaction of mayhem involving at least ten students, each of whom was torturing the one next to him or her in some way or another.

Great, I thought. *Maybe the Academy is just like high school after all.*

I pulled my eyes to the front of the Hall to see Merriwether walking to the center of a stage, with a series of faculty members seated in two rows behind him. The faculty, like the students, was dressed in color-coded outfits of red, green, and blue.

The Headmaster was the only one who didn't seem to fit into any particular group. He'd changed his clothes since our first meeting, and he now wore a long, tailored jacket of dark purple, a white, collared shirt, and pleated black dress pants. He still had on the same pair of combat boots, which gave his outfit the appearance of something randomly mashed together, and I giggled aloud at the idea of him as a banker moonlighting as a construction worker moonlighting as an absent-minded professor.

He really did have the air of a slightly off-kilter wizard. Except for the fact that in my mind, wizards were wizened old men, dignified and aloof. This man, with his patchwork of apparel, seemed like he was either too scattered to focus on fashion or else too serious to care.

Some of the men and women behind him wore pieces of armor along with their colorful tunics—silver steel shoulder pieces and ornately carved chest pieces, which I assumed indicated that they were fighters of some sort or another. Like Merriwether, some of them wore a cross between modern business suits and casual linen outfits, and I couldn't quite tell if they were getting ready for a board meeting or for war.

Their ages made it difficult to figure out where each ranked in the Academy's hierarchy. At first glance I spotted a few heads of white hair, but, at least from a distance, some of the faculty barely looked any older than I was. A young woman wearing a jacket, a pair of tailored trousers, and stiletto heels sat at one end of the front row. She reminded me of someone, though I couldn't put my finger on who, and I found myself studying her intently for a moment before shifting my attention to the students.

"The Blues are Casters. They're mostly magic users, Healers, anyone gifted in spell-craft," Niala told me. "Though some of the Zerkers use spells, too. The Greens are Rangers. Hunters. They go out beyond the Academy on scouting missions to track Waerg activity and anything else that might be a threat to the Academy."

I eyed Niala's blue waistcoat for a moment. "So, a Tethered is a magic user?" I said. "You're a Caster?"

"Rourke's not the result of a spell," Niala said with one of her silver laughs. "He's part of me, just like your hand's part of you. I'm only considered a magic user because I can heal myself and others."

My jaw dropped open. "You can?"

"No big deal. I mean, it comes in handy sometimes, but it's not like I've been on a lot of open battle fields to put it to the test."

"That's...pretty cool." *Understatement of the year.*

As I stared at the other students, I remembered that I was still wearing the clothing I'd put on that morning. All of a sudden, I felt horribly self-conscious in my jeans and hoodie.

"Don't worry," Niala said, reading my expression. "Everyone here already knows who you are. And believe me, what you're wearing is the least of their concerns."

Before I could ask her what she meant, my eyes landed on a tall young man who'd just stepped onto the stage. His hair was light brown and his eyes were so piercing that even from this distance, I could see how blue they were.

"Callum!" I whispered, fighting back a relieved smile. "He's here!"

"Surprised?" Niala asked.

"Yeah! I…I mean, I wasn't sure he'd make it. Merriwether—the Headmaster—said he'd be okay, but…it seems like everyone's surprising me these days. So, he's a student here."

"Callum's no student," Niala whispered with a wink. "He's what's called an Adjunct. He's not part of the faculty, but he helps them with the training. He knows everything there is to know about his particular…specialties."

A lot of what I'd noticed about Callum now made a certain amount of sense: His wisdom. His confidence. The authoritative voice and the way he carried himself. He may have looked seventeen, but he had a mien and a maturity about him that belied his apparent age.

"How long has he been here?" I asked, but Niala never got a chance to respond.

As I shot her a curious glance, Merriwether, who was still standing at the center of the stage, cleared his throat. In a deep, resonant voice, he called out:

"Welcome all, newcomers and established students alike, to the Academy for the Blood-Born!"

Any students who had been chatting or hitting each other suddenly clammed up, locking their hands in front of them.

"We are here today for many reasons, one of which is to extend a formal welcome to the thirteen Seeker Candidates who have recently joined us."

A polite, if unenthusiastic, smattering of applause rose up from around the room. I looked around, searching out the other Candidates, who had to be there somewhere. But I couldn't find them in the sea of students.

"It's been many years since we've had to call upon the Seekers," the Headmaster continued, "and the thirteen of you do us a great service by coming to the Academy. We all know how difficult it was to make the choice to leave your comfortable homes for a place so foreign and full of risk."

As he spoke, his eyes settled on the students sitting in the very front row of the Great Hall. I pushed myself up onto my toes to see they all wore fitted silver jackets that looked as though they were made of expensive velvet, a badge of some sort sewn onto the left arm.

"Those are the ones you'll be competing against in the Trials," Niala whispered, leaning in close. "Rather, they're the ones you're *already* competing against."

"Why are they separated from the others?" I asked, noting the several empty seats surrounding the twelve of them on either side.

"Because they're special. Or, more likely, because no one particularly wants to sit with them," she said with a frown. "Now let's be quiet for a second. We need to listen or Merriwether will have both our hides."

"For those of you who haven't spent much time in the Academy," Merriwether continued, "this room, of course, is the Great Hall. This is where you will eat and where we hold Academy meetings such as this one when necessity demands. We train in several locations throughout the Academy, but the primary location is the Eastern Courtyard. You can find maps in your books, or you can always ask for assistance if you require it."

Merriwether shifted his focus to the Zerkers at the back of the room. "I expect those of you with more experience here to serve as mentors, tutors, and tour guides for the new arrivals."

A few of the Zerkers exchanged rolled eyes and looks of irritation. A low rumble of complaints began working its way through the Great Hall, but Merriwether raised a hand, immediately silencing any naysayers.

"Don't mind them," Niala said, leaning in close. "It's in their blood to be difficult, and they have practically no control over their tempers. The Zerkers are mostly butt-muffins who hate everyone, even each other."

"Butt-muffins?"

Niala gave me a playful elbow to the arm. "You know what I mean. Just give them a wide berth, okay?"

"I promise."

"However distasteful the notion of Seekers may be to some of you," Merriwether continued, surveying the room with a haughty look of warning, "they're here for one reason only, and we should all be grateful. The Mistress is getting stronger every day, and the Relics of Power have faded. Only the Orb of Kilarin is still in our possession. The other Relics need to be found if we have any hope of stopping the Mistress before she becomes too powerful to hold back."

The faculty members on the stage nodded in solemn unison. I looked at Callum, who was watching Merriwether intently, his jaw clenching and tensing in a slow rhythm. I remembered seeing the look on his face when the man in the alley had mentioned the Mistress. His hatred had been palpable. Whatever vendetta he had in mind for the Usurper Queen had clearly returned full force.

"What most of you don't know," Merriwether said, his gnarled hands gripping the edge of the lectern, "is that we have reason to believe the Mistress has already acquired the first Relic of Power."

A communal gasp rose from the Great Hall. The entire concept of a tyrannical queen, of a magical world, of shape-changers, and mind-readers—it was still new to me. But I understood enough to know a gasp like the one I'd just heard was...not good.

An oppressive veil hung over the room, the quiet terror of uncertainty before a hurricane makes landfall.

"For that reason alone," Merriwether continued, "our

timetable has been accelerated. We will need to make our move soon. It is imperative we collect the remaining Relics as quickly as possible, though naturally, we will take all necessary precautions. The Seeker will be selected in the usual manner, and the accompanying team assembled."

He looked around the room, his eyes narrowing under his thick brows.

"Which means that everyone in this chamber will be under close scrutiny during the coming days. Our common goal is to defeat the Usurper Queen and to unseat her once and for all."

Shouts of "Hear, hear!" rose up around me. Students clapped approvingly.

Meanwhile, I began trembling like a leaf on a tree that's had too much espresso.

The only group to remain quiet was at the front of the Great Hall, the row of Seeker Candidates.

Staring, I assessed them one by one to size up my competition, at least as well as I could from behind. Seven girls. Five boys, one of whom was the hulking seven-footer I'd seen in the hallway.

One of the girls had long, wavy hair so bright red it might as well have been dyed with fresh blood. She turned to whisper something to the boy next to her. She was pretty, her features elegant, her skin like porcelain, and she held her chin high as though she knew full well she was the best-looking girl in her row. She reminded me of Miranda, the head of the Charmers at Plymouth High.

I disliked her immediately, though I chastised myself for it.

"As for the Seeker Candidates," Merriwether continued, turning to face the group of twelve, "You have all come here of your own volition. You are each aware of some of the risks involved. In the coming days, you will learn more, of course. For the Candidate who is chosen, grave danger is in your future. And on that happy note, it's time to formally introduce you to the rest of the Academy."

As he spoke, a hologram-like projection appeared over his head of one of the Candidate's faces. I recognized the tall boy with the long limbs whose face had apparently been captured at some point on camera, which made me wonder with horror if the hallways were full of hidden surveillance equipment.

A series of words flashed to life above his image.

Name: Crane Jenkins

The name suited him. He did have the appearance of a long-legged bird that might take off into the sky at any moment.

Hometown: Ojai, California

The same was displayed for each of the twelve candidates sitting at the front of the room. I tried my best to register all their names and places of origin, but by the time most of them had flashed onto the screen, I realized I hadn't retained much of anything.

The twelfth Candidate to be displayed was the redheaded girl, whose name was Oleana Grace. Her hometown, apparently, was New York City. She turned to look around the Great Hall when the image of her perfect face appeared, issuing a smug smile, clearly confident she'd be the one chosen in the end.

I was perspiring in fear, waiting for the huge image of my head to start hovering above the room. It was my nightmare to have everyone's attention drawn to me, hundreds of my peers scrutinizing me at once. But to my relief, the projections stopped with Oleana.

"We've only seen twelve projections," Merriwether exclaimed. "But there are, of course, *thirteen* of you." With that, he pulled his eyes to me, which drew looks from everyone in the room.

Okay, this was definitely worse than a projection. If ever there was a time I wanted to sink into a hole in the ground, this was it.

I found myself slouching into my hoodie, issuing a sheepish smile to the denizens of the Great Hall.

"Stand up straight. Don't ever let them see your weaknesses," Niala cautioned quietly as Rourke, still in his Husky form, crept over and gave my hand a reassuring lick. "Don't show your rivals that you're feeling overwhelmed, or they'll do their best to eat you alive."

She was right and I knew it.

I told myself to mirror the redhead's body language, lifting my chin and pulling my gaze away from the mass of curious stares aimed in my direction and up to Callum, who, thankfully, was smiling at me. That was enough to reassure me and take my mind off the judgmental leers of literally everyone else in the room.

"I'd like," Merriwether said loudly, "to introduce Vega Sloane. She's the last of our Candidates to arrive. I trust you will all make her feel welcome. She had her birthday just yesterday, so as you can imagine, this has been a little overwhelming for her. We appreciate her quick decision-making and willingness to help."

I wasn't sure if he was expecting a round of appreciative applause, but it didn't come. Instead, it was a shimmer of nearby whispers that met my ears. Looking around, I wasn't entirely sure where they were coming from. I was, however, sure I heard the words, "Mariah," "grandmother," and what sounded for a second like "traitor."

Merriwether explained that our first lessons would occur in the morning, starting with basic combat skills. "Some of you established students who are more experienced than others will be training alongside our Candidates," he said, shooting a look toward the group of Zerkers. "I know you'll enjoy showing them how it's done."

"Holy crap," I muttered under my breath as I stared at the students in red. Many of the boys were enormous, muscular, and daunting-looking. The girls, too, looked like they could snap me in half like a pretzel stick. "Really? We're fighting *them*?"

"They're less powerful than Waergs," Niala assured me. "But they fight like animals. It's good practice."

"Yeah, well, I'm pretty sure they want me dead just as badly as any Waerg does. Why does everyone hate the Seekers so much, anyway? Aren't we here to save the day?"

"Yeah. But everyone else trains all year round, honing their skills under extreme conditions. And then the Seekers swoop in every half-century and grab all the glory."

It was then that a woman who'd been sitting to Merriwether's right stood up. She was tall—at least as tall as Callum—and wore a chainmail tunic, leather pants, and bright red leather boots. She would have looked downright comical had she not been such an intimidating presence. Her dark, shiny hair was tied back in a high ponytail, her lips coated in red lipstick. Sleek, cat-like, and vaguely angry, she looked like a video game villain.

"My name is Lady Gray. I am a weapons specialist here." She shot me a look before pulling her eyes to the Seekers' row. "Each of the Seeker Candidates will learn weapons skills," she said. "Though you will soon discover that they aren't the only thing that matters in this place."

I found myself looking down at my fingers, which were intertwining nervously. Would I be tested on how I held my fork? Whether I talked in my sleep?

"Seekers, the next week will prove extremely difficult for you all," Lady Gray continued, her eyes moving from one face to the next. "You will be tested constantly. You will find yourselves exhausted by the time the Trials begin. Some of you *will* be injured—that's a promise. You'll be happy to know that no one has died during this early stage of training. Yet."

She pulled her eyes to one of the smaller female Seeker Candidates, who immediately sank into her seat as though the words themselves were enough to cut her deeply. She looked like she regretted her choice to come here, and I found myself wondering if she'd even *had* a choice. "Being a Seeker is a tall order, and not every one of you will be up to the task. I will see you all in the morning. Be ready."

"Thank you, Lady Gray," Merriwether said, stepping forward once again. "Lady Gray will be instructing the courses on daggers and short swords," he announced to the room. "Some of you are already familiar with her methods."

A low buzz arose from the Zerkers. "She does love the sight of blood," one of them uttered far too loudly from the end of one row.

"He's not wrong," Niala whispered. When I looked at her with horror, she shrugged. "You have to be a little psychotic to teach teenagers to stab each other."

"Mr. Drake," Merriwether announced, gesturing toward Callum, "will be assisting in the training for ranged weapons, as well as fire spells."

"Fire spells?" I whispered.

"That's for the Sparkers," said Niala. "The students who can summon and manipulate flame."

"Callum can teach that?"

"He knows quite a lot about fire, actually."

A memory rushed to my mind of him telling the man in the alley that he could burn him to a crisp.

As I thought about how many powerful people were sitting in front of me, a rush of terror swept through me. It wasn't so much a fear of being hurt as of failure. What if I wasn't good enough? What if I made a total fool of myself in front of Callum? It seemed silly, given how little time we'd spent together, but I couldn't bear the thought of losing his friendship—or whatever it was that we'd begun to forge—before I'd ever had the opportunity to get to know him better.

"With that said," Merriwether concluded, "you are all dismissed. Your classes begin in the morning. I'll be watching you."

As the students rose to their feet and began shuffling out of the Great Hall, I shot one final glance toward Callum, hoping to find a way to speak to him. But Merriwether, who had stepped down from the stage, was already making his way over to us.

"Niala, take Miss Sloane to see the crafters so she can be fitted with her gear," he said. "Quickly, now. Dinner will be soon, and she needs to be outfitted before she eats."

Niala nodded reverently.

I shot a look over to Callum, who'd been accosted by a male student who apparently had some pressing question about the belt he was wearing. I managed to catch Callum's eye for a moment before Niala reached for my arm and dragged me out of the room.

"Come on," she ordered, her voice sharper than usual. "We need to hurry."

When we were clear of the room, I turned her way and asked if everything was all right.

"It's fine," she said quietly, though I could sense a lie.

When we'd passed a small group of students dressed in blue and green, she reached out and stopped me, pulling me toward the wall. "Don't let them see you looking at Callum like that," she said. "It'll make things difficult for you."

"I was just trying to..."

"Your cheeks were going red, you were two seconds away from hyperventilating, and you generally looked like a smitten kitten," Niala shot back quietly. "I'm serious, Vega. If the others think you're a favorite of his or of Merriwether's, you're going to find your time here really unpleasant."

As if in reaction to what she'd just said, a trio of boys who'd been standing close by wandered up to us. The tallest of them was dressed in red, his hair tidily combed back, a smug expression on his face.

"So," he said. "Vega-freaking-Sloane, is it?"

His tongue dripped with disdain as he uttered my name, like it was the most repugnant thing he'd ever had to say. "You don't look all that amazing. Does she, boys?" With that, he turned to his chuckling friends.

"I've never claimed to be amazing," I replied. "So I'm not sure what your problem is."

"You do realize this is the Academy for the Blood-*Born*, right? Not the Academy for the Blood-*Polluted*? You're supposed to be invited based on your ancestry."

"My grandmother was a Seeker," I snapped.

"Your bloodline's tainted, thanks to your granny," the boy said, turning around and gesturing to his friends, who let out a series of hoots after what they apparently thought was a very clever insult.

The first boy spun around again to look at me, holding a hand out, palm up. Slowly I watched as he pressed the tips of his thumb and middle finger together. As he pulled them apart again, a series of sparks flared up, growing into a fireball hovering in the air over his palm. "Besides," he said, "I hear your specialty is doors. Good luck winning a fight against me with a flammable hunk of wood."

"Shut it, Larken," Niala snapped, even as Rourke let out a low growl. "You don't know anything about Vega's ancestry, let alone her skills."

"I know enough," the boy replied. "I know she should never have been invited here."

With that, he turned and left, his friends accompanying him.

A sinking feeling overtook me, my stomach flipping over on itself. "What's he talking about?" I asked. "About my bloodline?"

"Ignore him," Niala replied. "He's an ass. Come on, let's get you geared up."

Without another word, she reached out and took my arm, holding on tight as she guided me down the hall.

GEARING UP

When we arrived at a room with a brass sign outside that said, "Gear and Weapons," Niala nodded to me to head in.

"I'll see you in a little while. When the bell rings for dinner, come find me if you want someone to sit with."

After nodding my thanks, I pushed the door open to find a number of women scurrying around inside a small, dusty room. To one side was a clothing rack packed tight with leather tunics, linen pants, and leather boots, and to the other side was another rack lined with weapons, scabbards, horse saddles, and a bunch of other items I didn't recognize.

"Vega Sloane," a short, roundish woman said, striding up to me. It was impossible to tell her age from her face. She had wrinkles, yet her eyes and skin were bright, her cheeks rosy. She wore a long gray dress tied loosely at the waist with a leather belt, and she looked me up and down as she addressed me.

"Yes?" I replied.

"You're the last of them, eh? Mariah Sloane's granddaughter?" She narrowed her eyes in an indecipherable way before adding, "Come with me. Quickly, now."

She escorted me behind a tall screen that concealed me from

the other women who were milling about the room. "Stay here," she said. "I'll bring you your items."

I nodded silently and watched as she disappeared around the corner, returning a few seconds later with a pair of linen pants, a white tunic, and a pair of leather boots that seemed, miraculously, all to be the right size.

"These should fit. Your armor will go over top of them," the woman said. "Even if the clothes don't fit perfectly, the important thing today is that you receive what you need to start your training at dawn tomorrow."

"Dawn?" I gasped. To someone whose ideal sleep schedule involved getting up at the crack of noon, the word was a horror. "Seriously?"

"Get used to it," she snapped. "A Seeker doesn't keep an easy schedule. You never know when you'll be called upon. War doesn't allow for naps."

"Wait. Isn't a Seeker just supposed to find the Relics of Power? I mean, I knew we were doing combat training, but we're not actually expected to fight…are we?"

The woman shrugged. "A Seeker gets called upon to do whatever he—or she—must," she replied with a smirk. "But really, how should I know? I'm just the help. I don't go in for all of that fighting and hunting business."

With that, she left me to put on my new outfit. When I'd dressed, another woman in gray brought me to the weapons rack on the far side of the room. I thanked her and began assessing my options. A woman dressed in green held each weapon up for me to examine, explaining what they were.

"This one's for stealthier fighters," she said as she pulled the first dagger out of its sheath. "Of course, if you're the aggressive type, you can go with a trusty sword."

She pointed to a narrow but long blade that looked like it might drag on the ground if I actually wore it at my waist. "You also have the option of projectiles, of course."

I looked over at the next table, where an elaborate bow lay next to a quiver filled with arrows. They were certainly the most appealing option, given they would mean I could keep my distance from any enemy.

"So, you're thinking archery," the woman said. "Interesting."

"Why's that?" I asked.

"Because it was one of your grandmother's specialties. Along with daggers."

"You…knew my grandmother?"

"Don't let the youthful appearance fool you. Yes, I knew your grandmother. Very well. She was the best Seeker the Academy has ever seen. Oh, she had to make some difficult decisions when her time came to leave for good, but I've always admired her for it."

"What decisions?" It was the closest anyone had come to telling me anything about my Nana's time here.

With a frown, the woman shook her head. "It's best if you ask her yourself. It's really not my place to talk about others' lives. I probably shouldn't have said anything about it."

"Right," I replied, a wave of disappointment washing over me as I realized I was probably never going to learn the truth. "Of course."

When I'd selected a bow, a small dagger and a simple leather quiver, the woman assured me that all my new gear, armor, and other clothing would find its way to my sleeping quarters that evening. "Your weapons will make their way to the training grounds. You can keep on what you're wearing now," she told me, gesturing to the new linen tunic. "It suits you, actually."

I shot myself a look in a nearby mirror, only to see that my eyes, which had seemed to brighten the previous day, were now shining out from my face like two glowing hazel gemstones. Some sort of new life had sprung up inside me, and for the first time in a long time, I actually felt oddly pretty.

My mother would have been so happy to know it.

I thanked the woman, made my way out of the room, and headed back down the corridor leading to the Great Hall. But apparently, I'd gotten myself turned around, because nothing looked familiar. Frustrated, I wandered a little more until I came to an empty stone hallway filled with screens, which lit up as I moved, flashing the Academy's sigil: a silver sword on a white background.

It seemed the walls were trying to tell me something.

"Right, I get it," I said. "You want me to consult the book."

Seating myself on a nearby stone bench, I pulled my phone out of my satchel and flicked the button on its side. The screen flared to life. I was stunned to see the battery had survived this long, until I realized there was no icon in the upper right corner to tell me how much life was left in it. It seemed my phone was now feeding off some other energy source entirely, though I had no idea what it could be.

Sliding my finger along the glass screen, I scrolled through the book's cover and table of contents, scanning for any important chapters that could explain the basics of the Academy. Before I knew it, I'd read up on protocol for sleeping quarters, mealtimes, and a brief history of the Academy and its grounds. It was then that I came to a series of maps of each layer of the massive stone building.

You Are Here, a diagram of the main floor told me. Next to the words was a flashing red arrow.

Apparently, I was currently sitting in what was called the *Hall of Information*.

"Fitting name," I said as I looked around at the seemingly endless screens around me, which were suddenly displaying the same map. "But how do I get to the Great Hall from here?"

Almost immediately, a dotted line appeared on the maps projected on the wall-mounted screens, leading from my location to one several hallways away, and stopping at a large room at the west end of the Academy's main floor.

"Thank you," I said with a smile.

I shoved my phone into my bag, rose to my feet, and began the long hike back to the Great Hall, winding my way through the corridors as the map had told me to do.

Just as I came to the last large set of doors before the Great Hall itself, they opened to reveal Callum's familiar and strikingly handsome face. I was on the verge of saying his name when I froze in my tracks. Niala had warned me about interacting with him. Did that mean I couldn't even say hello?

As if in answer to the question, Callum gestured to me to tuck myself into a small alcove off the corridor, in between two statues of what looked like ancient kings.

"Hey—are you okay?" he asked when he'd joined me. "I wanted to ask you earlier, but..."

"I'm okay," I replied with a meager attempt at a smile. "A little confused...no, a lot confused. What happened to you in Fairhaven? How did you get away from...*them*?"

"I have my ways," he said with a quick grin, his eyes shifting to peer out toward the corridor. "Look, we can't be seen talking like this. It's not good for you. If they sense we're close..."

Close. It was a nice thought, to say the least.

"Yeah, Niala mentioned something about that," I said with a rush of blood to my cheeks. "She said I couldn't be seen as a favorite."

"She's right," he said. "You can't...even if you *are*. Look, you need to excel in this place, and I can't interfere with your progress. It's really important that you succeed."

"But you're an instructor," I protested. "Aren't you supposed to instruct me or something?"

"I'm a weapons trainer," he said. "An Adjunct. That's all I'm supposed to be. Listen, I have to go before someone finds us like this." He shot another glance out into the hallway before turning back to me. "I'll see you around, Vega."

"Wait," I said as he turned to leave, drawing his eyes back to mine. "I don't suppose you know anything about archery?"

He threw me a knowing look that came close to evolving into a smile. "I've shot a few arrows in my time. I promise I'll do what I can to help you. You know that. You don't know how badly I want you to come out on top."

"But what if I'm not good enough? What if I don't..."

I was interrupted by the Academy's bell chiming four times, which, according to the book, was the signal that dinner would soon be served.

"No what-ifs," he said. "Lack of confidence is not an option. Merriwether thinks you have it in you to be the very best, and the truth is, we need you. Even if some of the Zerkers want to be pricks about it."

"You noticed they have it in for me already, huh?" I asked with a grimace.

"Hard not to. They're a rowdy bunch. Really good at being angry all the time. I wouldn't pay too much attention to anything they have to say."

Just then, a group of students raced by the entrance to our alcove, a little too close for comfort. Callum backed into the hallway, distancing himself from me. "Come find me after dinner," he said quietly. "In the Grove."

"I don't know where that is," I said. I'd stared at every map in the book but never noticed any location with that name.

"Picture the perfect orange tree," he said with a wink as he flashed me a smile. "In your mind's eye, I mean. Something tells me you'll find it easily enough."

A second later, he was gone.

I FOUND my way into the Great Hall, which had transformed since the earlier Assembly into a high-ceilinged and seemingly endless dining room. What looked like sophisticated elegant silver light fixtures hung here and there, hovering above the tables. The tables themselves were draped with linens matching the colors of the uniformed students—red, blue, green and silver.

I eyed the silver table for a moment, wondering if I was bound by some kind of Seeker duty to eat there, before hearing my name being called from somewhere behind me. When I spun around, I was relieved to see Niala's smiling face as she gestured me over to where she and Rourke were sitting at the end of a Casters' table.

"Everything okay?" she asked. "You look...preoccupied."

"I'm fine. This place is just a lot to take in," I said as I took a seat next to her, not wanting to mention how eager I was to devour my meal and to see Callum again. I wasn't sure what I wanted more—answers to my multitude of questions, or the warmth and reassurance of his presence. Either way, my current greatest wish was to find my way to his side.

"Of course. It's a lot of information overload, I'm sure. You've had a long day."

A long day. Massive understatement. Just this morning I'd dropped Will off at the airport, and now here I was in some other place entirely, a place that didn't exist on any map I'd ever heard of. A place that boasted dragons and shape-shifters, kings, queens, and apparently, wizards.

"Yeah," I agreed. "It's been the longest day of my life, and it's not over yet."

"Well, the good news is that we'll be sleeping in the same dorm room," Niala said with a smile as she stroked her fingers over Rourke's head. He was still in his form of a black Husky, his bright eyes watching the floor in case anyone dropped a shred of their meal on the ground.

"Really?" I asked. "That's a relief. I mean, I don't know anyone else, and I get the impression that no one's particularly happy to have me here. Not even the Seeker Candidates."

"You're their stiffest competition. Of course they're not happy about your presence."

"I don't see why they're worried about me," I protested. "I have no idea what I'm doing. I'm supposed to be shooting arrows tomorrow and I don't even know how to hold a bow. Besides, like that Larken kid said, all I'm good for is summoning doors. I'm not exactly a great warrior or anything."

"Just make sure the arrow isn't pointed at your face, and you'll be fine."

I let out a chuckle that almost threatened to turn into a rolling sob. "Thanks," I said. "I needed that."

"Now eat and get out of here. I can tell there's somewhere you'd rather be, and I can guess why."

"It's that obvious, huh?"

"Yup," she said, shoving a forkful of potato into her mouth. "Just do yourself a favor and make sure no one sees you."

THE GROVE

When I'd scarfed down my meal of pot roast, potatoes, and peas, I excused myself to make my way out of the Great Hall and down a series of long corridors, trying to find any clue as to the location of the hidden grove Callum had mentioned.

"Orange tree," I murmured as I walked around, looking for any sign of an exit that might lead to a hidden courtyard. "Callum said I should look for the perfect orange tree."

I nearly kicked myself when I remembered he'd told me to picture the tree in my mind's eye. Of course. It was the same thing Merriwether had done to get me to open a door to the Academy's library. Envision the tree, summon a door, and easy peasy, I'd be in the mysterious Grove.

Only I wasn't convinced it would be so easy. For one thing, I had to make sure no one would see me doing it.

I strode down an empty hallway until I found a small, shaded alcove and glanced around to make sure no other students were nearby. When the coast was clear, I closed my eyes and pictured the tree. A perfect, narrow trunk leading to a series of branches covered with healthy green leaves and spherical oranges that looked good enough to devour—peel and all.

"Please, please work," I mouthed as the image solidified in my mind. "Please let me end up in the right place and not in the middle of Florida…"

When I opened my eyes again, a door stood in front of me, a fruit tree carved into its surface. "I'm getting better at this," I said under my breath as I pulled the dragon key from my chain, unlocked the door, pushed it open and walked through.

On the other side, I found a series of tidily-planted trees nestled among a sea of perfectly trimmed grass. As the door fizzled away behind me, I stepped forward, inhaling the scent of citrus wafting through the air in sweet waves.

The high walls of a courtyard rose up around me, lush green vines covering their surface. This place was such an odd mix of old and new, with its hovering lamps and its high-definition video screens…and this. The feeling I'd stepped backwards in time and come out in the Garden of Eden. Everything was pure and simple, and no amount of technology could possibly improve it.

After a little while I came upon the tree Callum had mentioned, right in the middle of the orchard. It looked like a painting, so symmetrical as to be unrealistic. Something about it stirred a quiet feeling of bliss inside me. No matter what happened after today, I told myself, this would be our secret place.

It really was perfection.

A soft rustling behind me made me spin around, my heart springing to action in my chest. I wasn't supposed to be here, and I had no idea what repercussions I'd face if Merriwether or one of the other instructors found me.

But the moment I saw who'd made the noise, I blew out a relieved puff of air. Callum was standing a few feet away, smiling broadly, unhindered now by the confines of what was deemed appropriate behavior between the Academy's walls.

"I'm probably an idiot for being here," he said. "I could get kicked out for less."

"So why did you come?" I asked with a smile, crossing my arms over my chest.

"Because I wanted to." He reached out and fingered the delicate tip of a nearby branch. He pulled his eyes to mine, and for a moment I was stunned to think I'd almost forgotten how brilliantly blue his irises were. "You look good in your new outfit, by the way," he said. "It suits you."

"Thanks. I usually stick to hoodies I can hide in, but I have to admit, I do like these clothes. They're the only thing in this place that feels really comfortable."

"I wish I could help you with that—with feeling comfortable, I mean. I know this must seem like a lot."

"I wish you could help make the other students hate me a little less. That would be a great start."

He shook his head. "They only hate what they think you are."

"And what is that, exactly? What do they have against my grandmother?"

Callum looked away, his jaw clenching. "I'm not sure I should tell you what I know. If Merriwether hasn't said anything, I probably shouldn't either."

"Please, Callum, just say it. I need to know what I'm up against."

He reached out and put a hand on my shoulder. I wasn't sure if it was to steady himself or me. "Some say she betrayed the Academy all those years ago," he said slowly. "After she found the Relics. Look, that's all I can tell you, because it's all I really know."

"Betrayed? I thought she helped. Merriwether said she was the reason the queen didn't rise to power sooner."

"Yes, that's true. Your grandmother did some great things. But people tend to forget the great things when there's a scandal involved. And rumor has it that her scandal was pretty serious."

Scandal. I pictured my Nana—my adorable little scone-making, scarf-knitting grandmother—and tried to imagine her embroiled in any kind of nefarious activities. It was impossible. As far as I knew, the worst thing she'd ever done in her life was accidentally spill some tea on one of her favorite lace doilies.

"I don't believe it," I said. "I don't believe my Nana would get up to…whatever she was supposed to have gotten up to."

"Good," said Callum, pulling back. "You shouldn't. Gossip is idiotic, not to mention pointless. Besides which, I have no idea what she was supposed to have done. So, let's talk about something else." He glanced around at our surroundings. "This place is too pretty to deserve negative talk."

"So what should we talk about?" I asked, relieved to drop the subject.

"What do you want to know? Ask me something. Anything."

I took a step toward him, pulling my chin up to narrow my eyes at his handsome face.

"I want to know you, Callum Drake. You're not what I thought you were when we first met, but I had a feeling about you."

"Oh? And what feeling was that, exactly?" he said, leaning toward me so that our faces were mere inches apart.

"I'm not sure. All I knew was that you didn't seem to belong in Fairhaven. You seemed…too regal. Or something. Like you should have been wearing armor and leading armies to war."

"Ah. I figured it would probably come down to this at some point." He was smiling again, but I got the impression that his eyes were hiding something. "Unfortunately, I can't tell you much."

"Okay, let's start with where you're really from. Because something tells me it's not England."

"I've spent a good deal of time in England, but it's true that I wasn't born there."

"So, you were born here. In the Otherwhere."

He nodded. "I'm from the region called Anara."

"The region with the green hills," I said. "The one I saw when I came through the dragon door."

"Yes. That's home."

"It's beautiful. I've never been anywhere so peaceful in my life. It's how I imagine a lot of the world—my world, I mean—was a long time ago. Yet it's so different." I cocked my head at him. "So the people Liv met—your parents..."

"Aren't so much my parents as temporary guardians, put in place by Merriwether."

"I see," I said. This was growing more intriguing by the moment. "I have another question, one that might end up making me feel pretty stupid, because you look young. But..."

"You want to know exactly how old I am."

"All I know is that nothing about you seems seventeen, except maybe your features. But even so..."

Callum chuckled. "People where I come from...we age slowly. So, technically, yes. I'm a bit older than seventeen."

"How much of a bit older?"

Callum seemed to hesitate. He pulled his gaze into the distance at a far wall covered in braided green ivy. "If I have to put a number on it..."

"Yes?"

"A *little* older than you. Or possibly a lot."

"Tease."

"Does my age matter to you?"

I shook my head. "You have this aura about you. Like you're some man of the world who's been everywhere, done everything. Seen lots of...people." I raised an eyebrow, curious to see if he'd realize I was talking about girls.

Callum caught my meaning, apparently, because he replied, "Not so much. You might be surprised to learn that I haven't exactly had much of a social life. I've been sort of busy with other things."

"You're telling me you've been walking around, looking like..." I gestured at him with my right hand, "...*this*...for ages, and you haven't had a thousand girlfriends?"

Callum snickered. "Not even close."

"That seems unlikely." I found myself pulling back and throwing up an emotional wall between us. I was beginning to wonder if I could trust him. There was so much he kept under wraps. So much he was unwilling to divulge.

"Vega, I'll never lie to you. You don't need to worry about me having wandering eyes, let alone a wandering heart."

Once again, he seemed to be reading my mind, or at least my mood. He slipped his fingers under my chin, raising it so that our eyes met. I considered pulling away, but instead I let myself savor his touch, studying his eyes to see if I could detect a lie in anything he was saying.

"Well, what you do with your time is none of my business, anyhow. It's not like we're..."

"Dating?" He pulled his hand away, dropped it to his side and chuckled. "No, I suppose this thing of ours wouldn't exactly fit the conventional idea of dating in your world or mine."

"Wait—this *thing of ours*?" I asked, my heart doing a little happy dance. "You're saying we have a thing?"

"I'm saying I have feelings for you. Feelings I'm not meant to have. I'm not talking about age now, because as far as I'm concerned, we're equals on that front. I'm talking about the fact that I'm supposed to be objective where the Candidates are concerned. Falling for you, it's inadvisable at best."

I felt the rush of blood to my cheeks at his words. *Falling.* Yes, that was what I'd done, too. He made me feel like the ground disappeared from under my feet every time I set eyes on him, like I was weightless, floating in a state of affection unlike anything I'd ever known.

"What happens if I don't make it here, Callum?" I asked.

"What happens if I fail...if I'm not selected? Will they just send me home, and that's that? I'll never see you again?"

He reached for a nearby orange and plucked it off its branch before playing with the peel. "Don't talk like that. You haven't even begun your training yet."

"But I have to prepare myself. What if..."

"Stop." His jaw was set now, his eyes flaring brighter as he set them on my own. "Don't. You have to be selected. You have to be the one they choose to find the Relics of Power."

"Why?"

"Because if you leave this place—if you're not selected, then you're right. There will be no us. And I don't want that any more than you do."

He played nervously with the orange's peel, slicing it open with his thumbnail. "I've never met anyone like you. In all my years, I've never met someone who struck me the way you did when we first met. There's something in you—something you don't see in yourself, which is endearing and infuriating at once. And it shines out like a light. Even your name glows, for God's sake; the brightest star in the Lyra constellation. You don't see your own beauty, whether it's internal or external. You don't see your own worth. But you need to start seeing them, or you'll be eaten alive in this place, and I couldn't bear that."

I thought of all the times I'd stared at myself in the mirror, all the times I'd scrutinized every individual flaw. I'd never seen myself as a bright star. I was the girl who walked around Fairhaven with her hands shoved into her pockets, hood pulled over her head. I was a girl who wanted to live in shadow, to hide from the world.

I wasn't sure I could see myself the way he did if I tried for a thousand years.

"I don't know what to make of you at all," I said, gesturing toward the walls, "let alone of this place. I just hope I can somehow live up to your high expectations of me." I turned away from him, fingering a leaf with one hand while I clenched the other into a frustrated fist. "Besides which, everyone here seems to want me to fail."

"Not everyone," he said. "Not me. Not Merriwether, or Niala. We're all rooting for you. Look, you didn't need to come here. You could have said no, handed the key to Merriwether and walked away. But you didn't. You're here, ready to sacrifice everything. And why? To help people you've never even met. Don't sell yourself short. You have no idea what you're capable of. You've only just found out that you're a Seeker. You just had your birthday. Your potential is still waiting to be unleashed."

I blew out a puff of air and turned back to face him. "Yeah, well, Niala has a changeable animal at her side at all times. Some of the Zerkers look like they could kill me with a stare. I may be considered athletic back in Fairhaven, but something tells me running the hundred-yard dash in the Otherwhere isn't going to win us any wars."

Callum let out a strange laugh. "Vega, if only I could tell you…" he said. "If only you knew…"

"Knew what?"

His face hardened into a frown, and I could see the young man who would train us in battle overtaking the boy who sometimes seemed on the verge of opening up to me. "If only you knew what you really are," he said.

"What am I?" I asked, edging closer to him. "Can you tell me that much?"

"You're amazing. In so many ways."

He stepped closer, slid the backs of his fingers along my left cheek, then pulled back suddenly, shaking his head as if to remind himself that what he was doing was forbidden. "You… you should go to the dorm. Get to know your peers. Who knows? You might actually like a few of them."

"I doubt that. I don't like anyone."

"You like Liv, don't you? Back home."

"Well, yeah. But she's everything I'm not. She's my better half. I don't need more halves."

Callum laughed. "Well then, you should look for allies here. You'll need them when the time comes. One day, you may find yourself relying on one of the Zerkers to save your life, or they may rely on you for the same."

The thought of it was overwhelming. Callum had rescued me, once from the odd woman in the park, once from the Waerg in the alley. But I'd never thought of myself as anyone's savior, and the idea of it seemed insane. But I nodded, nonetheless.

"All right," I said, stealing the now peeled and sectioned orange from his hand and popping a piece in my mouth. "I'll go crash out with my new buddies. I may as well get some rest before I get my ass kicked tomorrow."

"That's the spirit," Callum replied with a reassuring smile, taking a step closer even as I backed away. He reached out playfully and grabbed my left hand, pulling it to his lips. When he kissed it, I felt my center of gravity drop, my knees going soft, threatening to let me crash to the ground.

I was falling all over again for the boy with the bright eyes.

"When all this is over," he said, holding me in place, "when everything is as it should be...when you've been selected..."

"Yes?"

"We'll see." His smile told me he was as full of hope for us as I was, but neither of us was willing to say it out loud.

"We'll see," I said with a reciprocal grin.

With that, I turned and raced to the nearest door, yanking it open and stepping through.

THE DORM

THE DOOR I'D COME THROUGH DISAPPEARED WITHOUT A TRACE into the wall behind me, and as I looked for it, suddenly I understood why it was impossible to find the Grove. If not for the fact that I'd just been there, I wouldn't believe it actually existed.

Distracted by my bittersweet tryst with Callum, I started wandering. I must have looked lost, because as I was making my way along a main floor hallway a girl approached me, chin down, and addressed me. I knew before she spoke that she was a Seeker, by her silver jacket with a small embroidered sword on its left sleeve. As I eyed her, I recognized her as the mousy girl who'd shrunken into her seat during the Assembly.

"You're Vega, right?" she asked, her voice meek and timid.

"I am," I replied, trying my best not to sound cold as I spoke. "And you are?"

"Margaret, but most people call me Meg."

"Meg." I held my hand out and she took it with a grin that told me she was grateful to discover I wasn't going to bite her head off.

"Have you been here long?" I asked.

"Only a couple of weeks," she said. "I turned seventeen ages ago, but they only came for me recently." She shot me a look that told me there were multiple thoughts churning through her mind at once.

"Oh," I replied. "I assumed you'd all been here for months, training and whatnot."

"No. I mean, the rest of us Candidates have been here for a while, but we haven't done much training. I guess because they knew you'd be coming along...Do you want me to take you to the dorm?"

"That would be nice, actually."

Meg lifted her chin, her smile broadening, and she immediately seemed to acquire a skip in her step.

"I'm so glad you're here," she said as she led me down the hall toward a large black door I hadn't seen before. "People have been talking about you, but the way they talked, I assumed you were..." She slammed her mouth shut. It seemed she'd been on the verge of saying something potentially offensive.

"It's okay," I said with a chuckle. "I can take it."

"Well, I just figured you'd be some kind of monster. The way Olly was talking..." Once again, she stopped herself. It seemed Meg had a habit of divulging information that shouldn't be divulged.

"Olly?" I asked.

"You know. Oleana, the girl with the red hair. She comes from a long line of Seekers. Then again, I suppose we all do." Meg let out a sigh. "She's super-talented. She'll probably win this whole thing and get selected, then marry Callum Drake and live happily ever after."

"Wait—marry Callum?" I asked, my jaw tensing. "Does she have a thing for him?"

Meg let out a laugh. "Every girl in this place does. I mean, did you see him up there on the stage? When he showed up in my town, looking for me, I thought I was going to have a heart attack. I'd never seen a boy like him."

"He came to your town, too?" I supposed I shouldn't be surprised to hear it. He'd probably spent time with all the Seeker Candidates, sizing them up and watching over them as they turned seventeen. Still, the thought of it filled me with an envy I didn't particularly enjoy.

Meg nodded vigorously. "I couldn't believe a guy that handsome was there to hang out with me."

"He *is* handsome," I said through gritted teeth. "Well, I'm sure he and Oleana will be very happy together."

"I know, right? They'd have such cute kids." Meg let out a funny little laugh and led me over to a staircase at the end of the hall. As I suppressed the urge to gag, we climbed up to a narrow hallway with several doors on each side. "Anyhow, I'm so glad you're nice and not a monster. I really was worried."

"Glad to put your mind at ease."

"We're in twelve," she said, pointing ahead. "It's not just Seekers in our dorm room, either. There are some others in there —Zerkers, and a Caster or two."

"I heard."

Just as we got to our door, I took Meg's arm gently and stopped her. "Do me a favor, would you?" I asked.

"Sure, anything!"

"Don't tell anyone I'm not a monster."

Her eyes went wide before she narrowed them and gave me a knowing look and a broad grin. "Gotcha," she said. "Your secret's safe with me."

"Thanks."

The dorm room turned out to be remarkably modern and clean. Ten beds lined the two opposite walls, boys on one side, girls on the other. Light fixtures hovered above every bed, rising and lowering depending on the height of the student who used them. The beds themselves were modern-looking brushed nickel, with white linens and storage compartments underneath their frames. The floor was black, polished wood. One bank of windows looked out over the sea. On the other side of the room, a second row of windows looked down onto the courtyard far below where we'd be having our first weapons training session in the morning.

A few students were already sitting on their beds, either chatting or reading. The Zerkers in the room seemed to form a small clique, keeping to themselves in a far corner. The Seeker Candidates were more solitary, each occupying his or her own private island of a bed.

"Bathroom's at the other end," Meg told me as I stood by the door, looking confused as always. "You'll find a locker in there with all your gear."

"Thanks," I said, noting the white door at the far end of the long room. Getting to it would mean walking by all the other students, and the last thing I wanted was to draw attention to myself. But I didn't exactly have a choice.

I strode through the space, eyes focused on the door, which shimmied open on my approach. Inside I found what amounted to a large locker room, on the other side of which was a shower room, then a row of bathroom stalls.

Like the dorm, the bathroom was sleek and modern with a black granite floor and marble sinks. Everything was automated. When I so much as hinted that I needed water, the nearest tap turned on. When it came out hot, I said, "Cold," and the tap obeyed, offering a spring-like outpouring of fresh, frigid water, which I gratefully splashed on my face before dabbing myself dry with a plush, lavender-scented hand towel.

Next, I found the large locker with my name on it, written in delicate, scrolling script. Inside were my various outfits and a glowing screen that flashed images of toothbrushes, shampoo, deodorant, and any other necessity I could possibly want. I tapped the image of a silver toothbrush, and next thing I knew, I was holding one in my hand, my name engraved in its handle.

"This place is nuts," I said under my breath.

If it hadn't been for the fact that I fully expected to die a horrible and violent death in the near future, this would have felt like the most luxurious holiday I'd ever taken. The dorm was like one of those fancy hotels I'd seen in movies but had never been to in real life. I half-expected some snooty concierge to burst in and threaten to call security if I didn't leave immediately.

Among the clothing inside the locker was a set of silver satin pajamas, which I put on after taking a long, hot shower. As I looked at myself in the mirror, the Academy's sigil reflecting prominently on the breast pocket, I felt for the first time like I had a place here. I didn't know where the burst of confidence came from. Maybe it was the hot, cleansing shower I'd just had. Or maybe it was the need to get some answers—about my grandmother, about this world, and about myself. Either way, I told myself to forget about feelings of insecurity and self-doubt. I would do everything I could to come out on top, without worrying about making friends or securing enemies.

I was here to help the Otherwhere. To fight those who had killed my parents. To make the world a better place.

Surely, I could stand a little pain along the way.

I was relieved to see Niala walk into the dorm soon after I'd left the bathroom, gesturing me over to a bed at the far end of the room.

"Stay close to me. We'll be bed-neighbors," she said, nodding down the way toward the other Seeker Candidates, some of whom had arrived since I'd headed into the bathroom. When I turned to look, I could see that Oleana was sitting on the edge of a bed some distance away, staring out a window toward the sea far below.

I stared at her for a moment, ashamed to remember my earlier bout of jealousy. She was beautiful. It wouldn't surprise me to learn that Callum was interested in her. But the fact remained that I was the one he'd invited to the Grove. He'd chosen me to spend time with, not her. And for once in my life, I should recognize that maybe I was just a little bit special.

Rourke, who had turned into a small orange tabby cat, leapt up onto Niala's bed and curled up like a cinnamon roll.

"So, how are you feeling, anyhow?" Niala asked, perching on the edge of her bed and leaning toward me as I got ready to tuck myself in for the night.

"About?"

She gave the other end of the room a side-eyed look and nod before pulling her gaze back to mine. "The competition. How do they look to you?"

I looked over, assessing the group. On the boys' side of the room was a young man who was built like Callum but thinner, his limbs longer and more fragile-looking. He had strange eyes that seemed more caramel-colored than brown, and his skin was fish-belly pale. Another of the boys spent the entire time jotting something down in a notebook, which he tucked protectively under his pillow before yanking it out again to take more notes.

"I mean, I couldn't beat any of the guys at arm-wrestling," I said, eyeing the girls on our side of the room. "As for the ladies..." None of them had animal companions like Niala did, but a couple looked intimidating. One of them was taller than most of the boys, with a sweep of short, black hair and a face permanently set in an expression of rage. She didn't speak to anyone, instead spending her time assessing all of us for weaknesses. At least, that was what it felt like.

"That's Freya," Niala whispered. "She's a *Pathic*."

"I...don't know what that is," I replied.

"She moves things with her mind. I've seen her do it, even when she's not supposed to be using magic. Word has it she's not happy you're here."

"Great. Join the club, Freya," I moaned, my mind veering to thoughts of what Callum had said about wanting me to be selected in the end. How could that possibly happen? Every single person in this room was more powerful than I was. Every one of them, even the most unassuming-looking among them, could kick my butt to the moon and back. Even sweet little Meg was probably going to turn out to shoot bone-slicing laser beams with her fingertips or something.

"Don't worry," said Niala. "I'm sure you'll be fine."

"Uh-huh," I said, falling back onto my bed and pressing my head into my pillow. I covered my face with my forearms, wondering how I was ever going to make it through the next few days.

TRAINING DAY

AT SOME UNGODLY PRE-DAWN HOUR THE FOLLOWING MORNING, WE were woken by a woman in a long gray robe who stood silhouetted in the doorway with two fingers in her mouth and whistled loudly enough to shatter windows a mile away.

I shot bolt upright in bed, kicking and thrashing in my sheets, my heart threatening to explode as my mind struggled to remember why the heck I wasn't in my comfortable bedroom at home in Fairhaven.

Niala was perched on the side of her bed, already dressed and stretching her arms overhead while Rourke, who had transformed into his ferret form, let out an adorable but slightly terrifying sharp-toothed yawn next to her.

"Holy crap!" I hissed when the human alarm clock had left. "Does she wake us up like that every morning?"

"She sure does," Niala said, rising to her feet. "Now get your gear on. Remember, this morning is combat training."

I reached over and yanked my phone out of my satchel before reminding myself that it wouldn't tell me what time it was. I almost didn't want to know. I'd always been a morning person, as long as "morning" started at eleven A.M. or so.

I pulled myself to my feet and walked sleepily over to the locker room to grab the outfit the supply women had provided to me the previous day. When I had my gear in hand, I showered and changed as quickly as I could. Niala, who was still waiting when I came back out, accompanied me to the Great Hall, where we ate a breakfast of eggs, bacon, and toast. I savored it, all too aware I could die within hours in some horrible stabbing incident.

For the first time since my arrival at the Academy it hit me how much I missed Will. The comfort of his presence, his smile, his constant reassurance. I could have used some of him right now.

Feeling like a mountain-climber without a lifeline, I found myself looking around for Callum, hoping to spot him in the Great Hall before heading out to the courtyard. His smile was almost as reassuring as my brother's, after all…even if his presence had an entirely different effect on me.

As we ate, a series of floating projections appeared in the air above the tables. The repeated image of Merriwether's smiling face looked out over the Great Hall for a moment before he announced, "You have precisely ten minutes to finish your meal before you need to head to the courtyard. Be there and be alert. You will be working with actual weapons, which have sharp blades, in case you're unfamiliar with the large family of knives, swords, and other potential maiming devices. Enjoy your first official day of training. But be careful, all of you."

With that, the projection disappeared.

Breakfast helped wake me up a little, but most of the job was performed by the slowly-building adrenaline fueling my body. I couldn't help wondering what we'd actually be doing this morning. Fighting one another? Shooting at moving targets? Generally making idiots of ourselves?

"It'll be fine," Niala assured me.

"I'm that readable, huh?"

"You're tense. All the Seekers are."

I looked around, noting all the students in silver. She was right; every single one of them—even Oleana—looked like their bodies had turned into trembling stone.

"Glad I'm not the only one," I said. "Misery does love company."

I shoved the last of my food into my mouth and cleared my plate away.

"Come on," Niala said, following me to the door. "I'll show you the way."

I hurried to keep up with her, annoyed on the one hand with her speed and confidence but happy and thankful on the other hand that at least I had a guide in this odd and intimidating place.

The courtyard was expansive, gray, and somewhat grim. High stone walls thrust upwards on each side, punctuated by small windows here and there. It took me a moment to realize that the only students involved in our particular training session where the ones from our dorm room.

"Where's everyone else from breakfast?" I asked Niala.

"Probably gone back to their dorms. Most of us train year-round, so taking a beginner class isn't exactly needed."

"So why are you and the others here?" I nodded toward the students who weren't Seeker Candidates.

"We volunteered."

"That was nice of you."

"Don't get too excited. Some of the volunteers probably want to hurt you. This is their way to get easy access."

"Well, that's great news."

As Niala let out a laugh, Rourke transformed into his large black panther form. I eyed the cat, who let out low, luxurious purrs as she stroked his head.

"I like to be a little intimidating for the morning sessions," Niala confessed. "If we're going to fight, I don't want anyone getting any ideas that I'm a pushover."

"You definitely don't look like a pushover. I hope I don't have to spar with you two. I'm not sure this flimsy leather armor's going to be enough to keep his teeth from sinking into me."

"If you ever do have to fight us, I'll ask Rourke to change into a chipmunk," Niala replied with a wink.

"Gee, thanks. But he'll probably still find a way to nibble a hole in me."

"Chin up. I think this morning is just about learning to use the weaponry. You need basic skills before the real fighting begins."

She nodded over to a long rack set up along the courtyard's far wall, where someone had placed a series of weapons, including the bow and arrows I'd selected the previous day. "Come on, grab your gear. Let's see what you're made of, Vega Sloane."

But I hung back, watching as the other Seeker Candidates including Freya, the girl with the dark hair—the one Niala had said was a Pathic—made their way over and snagged whatever weapons they'd chosen.

Freya's was a set of two long, curved daggers that looked like they could eviscerate an elephant. As she walked back to my end of the courtyard, she clasped one dagger in each hand and shot me a look. Although no sound came out, the word she mouthed as she passed was as clear as day:

"Soon."

Nearly gagging on the softball-sized lump in my throat, I inched toward the weapons racks, my eyes darting back and forth as I waited for someone to scream at me that I was in the wrong place. When no one else paid any attention to me, I dashed over and grabbed the bow and a quiver of arrows, as well as the small dagger I'd selected the previous day, which I attached to my belt with the clip on its sheath.

"I feel so useless," I confessed as I moved back to Niala. The bow seemed brittle and weak, now that I compared it to some of the others' weapons. "I guess I should have asked for a semi-automatic machine gun instead."

"They don't have those here," she laughed.

"Why not? Seems like a smart alternative to spears and bows and arrows."

Niala laughed again, and I blushed so hot I thought my forehead and cheeks might melt.

"It doesn't work like that here," she said, waving her hand in the air and promising me she wasn't teasing me. "Everything you see here, everything you experience…it's all governed by old rules and even older magic."

"So I'll be okay with this thing?" I said, holding up the bow like it was a dead animal.

"Think of it like a can of mace, in case someone comes running at you."

"Great. If only I had this when I got dragged into the alley the other night. I could've sprayed a can of arrows in the guy's face."

Just then, a nearby door opened, and Callum and two instructors strode out alongside Merriwether, who positioned himself in front of the group of yawning and newly-armed students.

"This morning, you will be working in various stations in the courtyard," he announced, gesturing to several men and women in gray who'd just come out and begun to set up training stations. "Archers will make their way to the target row in the northeast corner. Swordsmen—and women, of course—will work with our training dummies. Those who want to learn dagger techniques will move onto that lesson when they've finished their first round. Now, head to your posts, and let's begin. Time is of the essence."

I shot Callum a furtive glance as I started heading toward the row of archery targets. In return, he threw me an almost invisible but reassuring nod before directing his gaze toward a small group of silver-clad boys who were off to the side, grunting under the weight of their thick broadswords. Although I kept a straight face, inside, I was cracking up laughing as I watched the humbled boys sway and stumble, the tips of the huge swords clanging on the ground. I didn't know much about archery, but if things got dangerous later on, I knew I'd be glad to have a weapon I could actually lift.

With most of the boys still staggering about and teasing each other for their pathetic efforts, the only boy who looked natural with his sword was Crow, who was holding a Tulwar, a curved sword I'd learned yesterday was lightweight despite the fact that it looked heavy and daunting.

Crow swung it around like he knew how to use it, his fierce eyes narrowed with focus. Clearly, he had grown up with a sword in his hand. As he approached the nearest human-shaped target mannequin, he took one swipe at its torso, slicing its burlap tunic in two before arcing the deadly blade around on the backswing and decapitating the helpless dummy.

"Holy crap," I muttered under my breath. "I wouldn't want to be on the receiving end of that."

"That's why you're wise to keep swordsmen at a distance," a voice said from behind me. I swung around to see Merriwether looking down at me, his fierce brows low over his eyes. "The secret is to stop them before they can come near you. Or, of course, to evade them entirely—which is a whole other set of skills."

"And what if I fail at both those things?" I asked.

"Then you're in trouble."

The softball in my throat returned, and I stared up at Merriwether, too petrified to form words.

"Would you like to know the secret?" he asked when he saw the look on my face.

I nodded, swallowing hard.

"All right then," he said softly, bending down so that his face was level with mine. "The secret..."

"Yes?"

"Is to always win."

With that infuriatingly vague and pointless piece of advice, he walked away.

Suppressing the urge to stick my tongue out at him, I made my way toward the target range, where one of the Zerkers was standing with a short bow and a quiver of blood-red arrows. He shot me a look before pulling an arrow out, setting it expertly, and firing it toward one of the targets.

When it hit dead-center, I nearly succumbed to the temptation to throw down my gear and yell out, "Okay, everyone, it was great to meet you, but I'm out of here!"

"Things are not looking good," I mouthed. I drew an arrow out of my quiver and tried in vain to position the small opening at its base against the string of my bow. As I struggled, I spotted a tall figure striding up. I could all but feel Callum's heat as he approached, and I was grateful for the comfort of his presence.

Even if I was about to make an idiot of myself.

"Let me help you," he said softly.

"Do I look like someone who needs help?" I asked as the arrow clattered to the ground at my feet.

"Yes. You really, really do."

He was holding a bow of his own in hand and drew it in front of his chest before guiding me through the steps.

He began with what he said was called "nocking" my arrow, which meant positioning it so that the bowstring slipped into the small opening carved into the shaft. He showed me how to aim and to position my shoulder and arm at the ideal angle, before finally loosing his arrow at the target.

Like the Zerker's, his arrow hit dead center.

"Impressive," I said. "It's almost like you've done this before."

"A few times, maybe. Now you try."

I did as he asked, carefully positioning my arrow—a process that took so long a herd of very slow-moving hippos could easily have taken me out before I got a single shot off.

After carefully setting myself up, I fired, missing the target by at least a foot.

"Well, it's a good thing there wasn't a baby goat standing next to it," I said. "Though that would've been just my luck."

The truth was, I wanted to punch a hole in the wall. I wasn't accustomed to being horrible at anything. And I definitely wasn't used to being the least talented person in a place full of teenagers.

"Is it frustrating?" Callum asked.

"Is the ocean wet?"

"Don't worry about it," he said, leaning in close. "Chances are, you'll never use a weapon, Vega."

"What? Are you serious?"

"I probably shouldn't say this, but Seekers generally don't fight—not exactly. There's a reason they get a whole team of protectors who go along for the ride. Seekers are here for their minds, not their physical talents. Besides, we don't really know the extent of your summoning power yet. You may find it's enough on its own to defeat anyone."

"Still, I'd like to at least be able to *pretend* I can hit something with an arrow. Right now, I feel like a total doof."

"Then here, let me show you," Callum laughed, grabbing another of my arrows and handing it my way.

He sidled up and positioned himself behind me, guiding my hands and arms from behind with his own. If he'd been anyone else, I probably would have snarled at him for patronizing me. But it felt too good to have him standing so close, to have his warmth and size engulfing me as they were. I liked the feeling of his fingers slipping their way down my arm to my hand as he told me what my wrist should be doing. I liked his scent, his voice, his everything.

But most of all, I liked feeling he had faith in me.

I tried my best to listen to his instructions, though admittedly I was a little distracted by his proximity. It was only when he moved away that I managed to focus my attention on the target.

His instruction, it seemed, actually paid off. I was able to hit the outer ring.

"There, you see?" Callum asked, stepping back.

I turned his way to shoot him a smile, only to see Merriwether standing in the distance, eyeing us with a stern expression.

"I think the Headmaster suspects we're closer than we're meant to be," Callum said softly. "I'd better see to the others before I get you sent to detention."

"Wait? They have detention here? I would've thought they'd just throw the bad kids into a pit of poisonous vipers or something."

Callum lowered his chin and shot me a "Really?" look before walking over to the dagger station, where Niala was attacking a target dummy from behind while Rourke, in the form of a snarling hyena, leapt at its throat.

I kept working on my shot, which improved gradually—that was, until it eventually became worse as my arm began to weaken from fatigue.

"Come on, Vega. I'm pretty sure tired arms don't work as an excuse in war," I mumbled.

It seemed I wasn't cut out for combat.

Then again, maybe I wasn't cut out to be a Seeker at all.

COACHING

WE SAT DOWN TO LUNCH AROUND ELEVEN A.M. AFTER A GRUELING morning spent shooting, stabbing and slicing inanimate objects. I found myself seated next to Niala once again, grateful for her and Rourke's company and for the food I was handed the moment I sat down.

"First sparring session this afternoon," one of the nearby Zerkers, a boy called Spiker, announced, shooting me a look. "I hope I get to go after Sloane. I'd take her down in three seconds."

The boy next to him laughed, slapping him on the back as if he'd just come out with some exquisitely witty insult.

I glared at him, lacking as I was in any kind of retort. The truth was, he was right. He probably could kill me with a single punch.

Well, at least he'd be putting me out of my misery.

When we finished eating, we headed back to the courtyard to work on hand-to-hand combat. Lady Gray and Callum coached us, demonstrating maneuvers to employ if ever we found ourselves under attack without weapons.

As they spoke to the group, another young man moved around the courtyard, nailing four posts into place before winding a rope around them to create a sort of makeshift wrestling ring in the center of the outdoor space.

The techniques Callum and Lady Gray demonstrated were impressive and mostly involved either aggressive punching, or else twisting themselves around like pretzels before throwing one another to the floor. They made it all look easy and fluid, but I knew full well that if I'd tried either move on someone their size, I probably would have been swatted away like an irritating gnat.

The first students called up were Crow and a boy called Nevin who was taller than his opponent, but less powerful-looking. From what Niala whispered to me, though, he had a gift for haste, so I supposed their match-up was a relatively fair one.

"Crow is many things," Niala said, "but fast isn't one of them."

As the two boys stepped into the ring, Callum explained the rules to them.

"Your goal for today is merely to incapacitate your opponent —not to injure them. Get them into a helpless position. Pin them for a three-count. You're here to show the Seekers how it's done before they have their turn. For those of you who are magic users," he added, turning to the group of thirteen moderately terrified-looking Seeker Candidates, "You may use your skills. But if one of you tries anything that breaks the Academy's rules, you will suffer the consequences. This is not the real world. In the real world, you will be contending with Waergs and other beasts. They won't fight on your terms for a second, so don't show mercy when the time comes. For now, however, I'd like you to start slow. We'll have plenty of time over the next week to practice giving and receiving some more serious strikes."

The only Candidate who didn't look frightened about what was to come was Freya, the dark-haired girl who looked like she wanted my head on a platter. I could have sworn I smelled bloodlust on her, if such a thing was actually smellable.

Callum backed away, signaling Crow and Nevin to begin, and

I watched as the two boys circled inside the ring like animals, sizing each other up for weaknesses.

It was Nevin who lunged first, reaching out long jabs and slashes at Crow, who barely avoided his opponent's claw-like hands.

Crow threw himself at his opponent's knees, driving him to the ground before Nevin executed some sort of blindingly fast spinning move, twisting himself free, leaping back to his feet, and darting to the far corner.

Crow wiped his mouth with the back of his hand, already irritated that someone had gotten the better of him. His chin tucked into his chest, his fists coiled in front of his face, Crow moved forward, a predator stalking its prey. Nevin, despite the fact he'd already hit the ground once, didn't look like he was planning on being anybody's punching bag.

As Crow unleashed a series of jabs, Nevin ducked, dodged, and weaved as the vicious strikes whistled harmlessly past his head.

With Crow's right side exposed, Nevin delivered a monster forearm strike followed in quick succession by two stinging jabs to Crow's rib-cage. Down on one knee with his head sagging, and clearly shocked by this sudden turn of events, Crow prepared for Nevin's final strike.

Except it never came.

As Nevin cocked his fist for an uppercut, Crow whipped his leg around, catching Nevin just behind the heel. Nevin cried out and flipped over backwards and, before I could even blink, Crow was sitting on Nevin's chest, knees pinning his arms helplessly to the ground, his hands clamped around his opponent's exposed throat.

Nevin gave a whimper and a tap to Crow's leg indicating his surrender. Some of the boys cheered while the others, Nevin-supporters apparently, grumbled and cried foul.

After everyone had calmed down, the other non-Seekers followed in groups of two.

When it came to Niala's turn, she was up against a Sparker who got two fiery shots off before Rourke, in panther form, incapacitated him by clamping his mouth over both wrists at once and sending the boy into fits of tortured screaming. Niala stood back, examining her nails casually as the crowd cheered.

To my horror, I was the first of two Seekers to be called up.

To make matters worse, Lady Gray assigned Freya as my sparring partner.

"But she can throw objects with her mind," I protested.

"You can summon doors," Lady Gray replied. "You seem like a perfect match, actually."

I shot Callum a look, to which he responded with a "What can I tell you?" shrug. He looked relaxed enough, so I told myself not to worry. There was no way he'd let me walk into a situation that was truly dangerous.

Would he?

Freya looked like she was out for blood. My blood. My only hope was to lunge at her fast enough so I could take her down before she managed to fling anything at me.

As we sized each other up, I began the session with a small dash of hope. I circled the ring, forcing her to move with me while I assessed the best way to tackle her. But it wasn't long before she stopped, a fiendish smile on her lips.

"Bash her head in!" Spiker yelled, to the jeers of his friends.

I spun around just in time to see a large rock flying at my chest. With no grace whatsoever, I flung myself out of the way as the rock went crashing to the ground a few feet away. *Crap.* I winced my eyes shut, all but defeated. Even if I could summon doors at the drop of a hat, there was no way I'd be able to do it fast enough to defend myself against another attack like that.

I was doomed.

Still, a shot of searing rage worked its way through me as my competitive side kicked in.

"You could have killed me!" I snarled, leaping to my feet and throwing myself at Freya.

I managed to knock her down before a large metal bucket came barreling through the air and hit me square in the shoulder. I staggered off her and to my right, clutching my left arm in agony.

"I said don't kill each other!" Callum shouted from the sidelines, but Freya didn't seem to want to heed his command. As I stared at her, something in my peripheral vision rose into the air, floating some distance away.

Horror worked its way through me as I turned and identified the object as a large mallet.

"Crap!" I blurted out as the mallet began its spinning flight toward me. I didn't have time to duck or to summon a protective door. All I could do was slam my eyes shut and hope I didn't die.

For a reason I couldn't possibly explain, one word flashed through my mind in that moment:

"Vanish."

It was then that two things happened: one, I opened my eyes to see that the mallet had landed on the other side of the ring, and two, a series of horrified gasps rose up around me.

I've died, I thought. *They're freaked out because they watched me die.*

It seemed, however, that I was wrong.

"A Shadow," one of the Zerkers shouted. "She's…a freaking Shadow!"

"That's impossible," another student said. "The only people who are Shadows are the masters of the Old Magic. Besides, she's a Summoner. She can't be both."

I turned, staring at the faces surrounding me. Each mouth was open in shock. Every set of eyes was open wide and darting around, scanning the sparring ring. Even my opponent was glancing around, too stunned to continue her onslaught.

"Liam is right," Lady Gray said, taking a step toward me. "Whether or not it makes any sense, Vega Sloane seems to be…a Shadow."

A sudden movement in a window above the courtyard drew my eyes upwards. I looked up to see Merriwether leaning out one of the narrow windows, staring down into the ring.

He was the only one who didn't look shocked.

"What are you talking about?" I asked, my voice turning quickly into a sob. "Someone, please tell me what the hell is happening!"

"Vega, look at your hands," Niala said, taking a step toward me, Rourke at her side. She looked like she was trying to focus on my face but couldn't. Even as she stared at me, her eyes moved around like she was following the trajectory of a bouncing ping-pong ball.

I pulled my eyes down to see that my hands were…gone.

Only they weren't, not exactly. They were a sort of translucent, swirling purple, like I'd turned into smoke. I could see them like vapor in front of me, but each time I tried to focus on some part of myself—my forearm, my finger—it seemed to disappear from view.

"What the—?" I choked out, pulling my eyes to Callum's. I knew how frightened I must look. How confused.

Except for the fact that he probably couldn't actually see my face.

"Breathe," he said softly, his eyes searching for mine. "Just breathe."

I did as he said, inhaling deep into my lungs before pushing out a slow exhalation. I found myself tumbling to the ground, landing with a soft thud, the earth puffing out from under me in gentle waves as if a whiff of air had disturbed it.

Sitting there, I watched as my hands slowly turned solid

again, my flesh returning to its proper mocha shade. I'd never been so happy to see my own skin.

"I'm sorry," I muttered to no one in particular. "I'm sorry. I didn't know I could do that."

"Didn't know?" Freya snarled. "As if you wouldn't know a thing like that!"

"Shut it, Freya," Niala shot from the other side of the rope barrier. "Can't you see she's freaked out?"

"The mallet…it went right through her!"

"If it hadn't," a deep voice said from somewhere behind me, "it would have killed her, and you know it. I want to see you in my office in five minutes."

I twisted to my right to see that Merriwether had stepped into the courtyard. The look in his eyes was pure rage, and the power in his voice was unmistakable.

"But…" said Freya. "You told me when we first met that this was a competition, Headmaster."

"A competition to prove yourself worthy. You failed. Now get moving!" Merriwether shouted.

Freya pushed herself to her feet, a surly look in her eyes as she glared my way.

"Vega," Merriwether said, "You're dismissed from this training session. I'd suggest that you make yourself scarce."

Niala and I shot each other an *uh-oh* look before I managed to scramble to my feet and slip under the ring's rope. I glanced over my shoulder at Callum, whose face told me he was almost as tormented by what had transpired as I was.

"The rest of you are dismissed, as well," Merriwether announced.

A chorus of disappointed moans rose up behind me as I left the courtyard.

Great. I'd ruined everyone's sparring fun, as well as turning myself into even more of a pariah than I already was.

My first full day at the Academy was going fabulously.

TRUTH

Instead of hanging around where I risked running into the students from the sparring session, I grabbed a dry bun and some butter from a cart at the entrance to the kitchen, ducked into a dark alcove, and summoned a door to the Grove.

I wasn't entirely sure I wanted to risk seeing Callum, but it was the only place where I could possibly be alone.

I couldn't seem to rid myself of the pained look Callum had in his eyes when I'd left the courtyard. The look of someone who was horrified by what he'd seen. He'd looked disgusted, even. I could only imagine that he thought I was some kind of awful aberration.

More than anything, I felt embarrassed, as if I'd had a dream I shouldn't have had and everyone in the entire Academy had been party to it. I'd been stripped naked in front of the world, only to have the world point out what a freak I was. By now, everyone in the entire Academy probably knew what I'd done. They knew I possessed some dark power that no proper Seeker was supposed to possess.

I sat on the grass, my back against the narrow trunk of a lemon tree, and ate my meager dinner, all the while feeling like a reject. Being ostracized from society wasn't exactly a new sensation, but somehow it felt worse in the Otherwhere than it ever had in Fairhaven.

At least in Fairhaven, I had my house to escape to, a room of my own to conceal myself in. Here, I had no choice but to be around other people. And to make matters worse, some of them already despised me.

"Penny for your thoughts?" a voice said, stirring me out of my self-pity fest. A frown crossed my lips as I turned to see Callum walking toward me, his hands behind his back.

"You're telling me you carry change?"

"I'm embarrassed to admit it," Callum replied, circling around to sit down in front of me. "But I don't have a penny to my name. How about this instead?"

He took his hands from behind his back and handed me a long-stemmed rose, its petals practically glowing a deep crimson red.

I took the rose from him and breathed in its heavenly aroma, relieved that Callum, unlike so many of my fellow students, wasn't horrified with me or off somewhere cringing in disgust at what I'd done back in the courtyard.

"It's beautiful," I sighed.

"So...about that thought."

"Well, let's see. A bunch of students already hated me. But now they hate me even more, because..." I stopped myself, worried my voice would crack.

"Because, as it turns out, on top of being a Summoner, you're also a Shadow," Callum said.

I nodded miserably. "Whatever that actually means."

"It means you're amazing," he replied.

I summoned the courage to pull my eyes to his, only to see a smile that told me he was proud of me for some insane reason.

"If I'm awesome, why were they looking at me like that?" I

asked. "Like I was this horrible creature who was going to eat their faces?"

"Because it scares them to see," he said. "Shadows are rare, and people associate them with rogues, assassins, and with the most powerful magic-users in the Otherwhere, not with newcomers to the Academy, and certainly not with Seeker Candidates."

"Well, I have no idea where this lovely gift comes from," I said. "It's not like I've spent my life around these masters of the Dark Arts."

"There's another reason the students were acting weird."

"Great."

"The fact that you can summon and take on a Shadow form—it means you're what's called a Multi."

I stared at Callum, overwhelmed by yet another curve ball thrown my way. What on earth was a *Multi*?

I'd been there less than two days and already my head was reeling, I couldn't get a straight answer out of anyone, and a fist-sized knot had taken up permanent residence in my gut. In a ridiculously short time, I'd gone from being the epitome of boring to the incarnation of freakish.

Two days before, I was the nobody girl in the shadows. Suddenly, I had a spotlight on me and a group of repulsed kids staring at me like I had two heads. I wanted to scream, growl, cry, curl up into a tight ball, and run away, all at the same time.

Callum must have sensed my anxiety, because his voice dropped and slowed to a molasses crawl.

"A Multi isn't a bad thing. It's just someone with more than one magical ability. Very few people are Multis. Only the most skilled in the Otherwhere. People like Merriwether and the Crimson King, back when he was alive. They say it can happen when one is a descendant of both a Seeker and a magic user—two parents, one from your world, one from mine. It's a hereditary thing, like having hazel eyes."

He gave me a wink then. It was funny—my eyes *were* hazel

once. But they seemed to change all the time now, varying from green to brown to blue and back again, depending on my mood.

"My father had blue eyes," I said. "My mother's were dark brown."

"And they combined into something beautiful," Callum replied.

"Well," I said with a flush of my cheeks, "my grandmother was obviously a Seeker. But my grandfather was a fisherman from Cornwall. So you're saying there was someone else in my ancestry?"

He nodded. "There must have been. Which is rare."

"Why's that? I would have thought magic users got together all the time."

"They do. But not with Seekers."

All of a sudden, I understood.

"Seekers can't stay here," I said. "That's what you mean. They don't marry people from the Otherwhere—they don't have children together."

"Right. They come to the Otherwhere, perform their duties, and leave when they've finished," Callum said with a nod. "Most Seekers, as I understand it, go on about their lives back in your world. They leave this place behind forever. It's always been the way."

"That's what my Nana did. She walked away and married my grandfather. And he was no wizard, except when it came to catching Atlantic salmon."

Callum went silent, a strange look in his eye.

"What is it?" I asked. "What is it that everyone knows but refuses to tell me?"

He pressed his hands into the grass and leaned back on his arms, inhaling a deep breath. "I asked Lady Gray about the rumor about your grandmother, the one that says she betrayed the Academy."

"What did she tell you?"

"She said that somewhere during the process—while she was recovering the Relics—she met a man. One who worked for the other side."

I froze. All of a sudden it all made sense—the hatred, the looks, the disdain.

My own grandmother had fallen for the enemy?

"I don't believe it," I said. "I can't..."

"I don't really believe it either. But I remember hearing whispers about it, even back when I lived in Anara. I remember the stories about the Seeker who left in shame after the portals had been sealed. She had issued an apology to the Academy and walked away, never to be heard from in the Otherwhere again."

"You think...you think the man she knew back then..." I began, unable to finish.

"Was your grandfather? What do you think?"

I didn't need to think about it. I already knew the answer. My grandmother had gotten together with a powerful magic user. Someone cruel, malicious. She'd fallen for the enemy, gotten pregnant, then returned to Cornwall, met my grandfather, and covered up the whole thing.

"But wait. My father never used magic," I said. "Wouldn't he have shown some signs?"

"Not necessarily. Like so many hereditary traits, magic can skip generations. Besides, your grandmother may well have tried to turn him away from it. Maybe she didn't want him to end up suffering the same fate she did."

"If she wanted to discourage him, she had a pretty funny way of doing it," I said, recalling her strange cottage in Cornwall, with its creepy objects and potion-like vials. The place practically screamed magic. Then again, maybe she deliberately exposed him to thoughts of magic and witchcraft as a means to make him rebel against it. My father was a kind, sweet man who was strait-laced to the core. Nothing about the occult or the paranormal had ever interested him in the least. At least not as far as I knew.

"Look, Vega," Callum said, leaning forward, crossing his legs and staring into my eyes, "there are always going to be people who don't like what you are. That's what happens to those with extraordinary powers. Trust me, I know."

"But how could you know? You never..."

I bit my lip when I realized I was about to point out that he never displayed any powers. I hadn't seen any sign that he was anything more than Callum Drake, the very handsome, very intelligent instructor.

"I keep my cards close to my chest," he said. "There's a reason for that. I'm sorry—I wish I could say more, but I can't."

He looked sad for a moment, but it passed. "Just do yourself a favor and try to embrace who and what you are. Whoever your grandfather might have been doesn't matter, because like I said, you're...amazing."

"I'm a freak."

"Fine. But you're an amazing freak."

We exchanged a quick narrowing of the eyes, then burst into laughter. It was the first time in what felt like ages I'd let myself laugh, and it felt good.

For the next two hours we lay in the grass, staring up at the sky and talking about Callum's world and mine, about our hopes for the future, about everything except for fear and doubt.

"I should probably head to the dorm," I said at last, pulling myself to my feet. "I'm sure my peers will want to gawk at the demonic beast I've become."

"Nah. It'll be fine. They might even surprise you, you know."

"Or they might murder me," I said with a wink. "It's been nice knowing you, Callum."

"Silly girl."

"Silly boy."

With that, I smiled and took off to see what my ridiculous fate had in store for me next.

SUMMONS

When I got to the dorm, I pushed the door open and strode through with as much confidence as I could muster, only to find an unexpected scene unfolding in front of my eyes.

The Zerkers, who were congregated in a far corner, chatting amongst themselves, turned to look when I entered the room. Some of them appeared frightened, their backs hunching the moment they saw me. They reminded me of a dog I'd once seen getting swatted on the nose for digging up its owner's garden. Cowering, confused, slightly terrified.

The only one who didn't look scared was Crow, who was standing on his own by the window. He nodded respectfully to me, and I thought I detected a slight smile.

The Seeker Candidates, on the other hand, sat on the other side of the room. They'd pushed their beds together and were squeezed in close to one another, having an intimate conversation.

Niala sat on her bed, with Rourke by her side. He was in his canine form, and her hand was buried deep in his fur.

When I headed her way, she said, "I think you should go make nice with your fellow Candidates."

"Oh? Why?" I asked.

"Just...trust me."

Taking a deep breath, I did as she suggested and headed over to where they were sitting. They lifted their eyes to stare at me. If the Zerkers were frightened of me, the Seeker Candidates looked impressed, even in awe. Even Oleana, who'd only ever looked at me with disdain, wore an expression that told me she was eager to talk to me.

"How did you do that?" she asked as I came near. "The Shadow thing—that was amazing."

My lips twitched into a smile. "I'm not so sure about that. There are people here who can shoot fire with their fingers. All I did was disappear—it's what I've done my whole life."

"Well, it was a cracking trick," said a boy with dark hair and rosy cheeks. His accent sounded English.

"Thanks," I said. "Honestly, all I know is I was afraid for my life."

Meg, who was sitting closest to me, moved over and patted the mattress next to her. I took the cue and sat down, looking around at the other Candidates.

"It was painful," I said. "Scary, too. I felt like something had been torn away—my flesh and bones, all at the same time, if that makes any sense. Like the only thing left was my mind."

"Well, if it makes you feel any better," Oleana said, "I don't think Freya really wanted you dead."

"The mallet she flung at my head would beg to differ," I replied.

"Freya really wanted to win. I heard her talking one day about the great Mariah Sloane..." She shot me a glance that told me she wasn't sure it was okay to mention my controversial grandmother before continuing. "She said her mother used to tell stories about Mariah's accomplishments as a Seeker. But the thing is, her mother has never been supportive of Freya herself. She puts her down, tells her she's terrible at everything."

"So you think Freya was just trying to prove herself?" I asked.

Oleana nodded, her red hair bobbing in waves. "I think she wanted to make her proud. She got carried away. I'm not saying what she did was okay, but I don't think it was out of spite. More like desperation."

"She'd probably heard the prophecy," the dark-haired English boy blurted out.

"Prophecy?" I asked, my brow furrowing.

"You don't know?" asked Meg.

I shook my head. "I've never heard anything about a prophecy."

The other Candidates shot one another a look before Meg finally spoke up. "They say the Crimson King's heir is still alive, and that he—or she—will come back someday and take the throne from the Usurper Queen."

"There's an heir?" I asked. "But I assumed..."

"That she killed whoever the heir was?" Meg asked. "We did, too. But I heard Lady Gray talking to another instructor about it the other day. She said she thinks you're the one who's supposed to help the heir find his way back to the throne."

"Why me?" I asked.

Meg shrugged. "Something to do with your bloodline."

I waited for her to expand on the thought, but she didn't. I shot a look toward Oleana, expecting the same haughty look of entitlement I'd seen the previous day, but I didn't get it. Instead she nodded reverently in my direction.

"If it's you," she said, "it's well deserved. I mean, I really wanted to be the one. But I can't compete with your abilities. No Seeker has ever been a Multi before."

I eyed her, trying to detect a hint of sarcasm, but there was none. I was beginning to feel bad for judging her so harshly. I'd assumed the worst about her, all because I figured she was cut from the same cloth as Miranda back home. But maybe she was more like me—someone who wanted to excel but who had been thrown into the deep end, only to realize she couldn't swim all that well. The Academy had a way of humbling even the most confident student, after all.

It was so strange to be sitting there with eleven sets of eyes fixed on me, eleven faces awaiting whatever I was going to say next. Everyone was paying attention to me.

And for once, I didn't mind.

"I appreciate everyone's faith in me," I said. "I really do. But we're all in this together. So let's keep training and see what happens. No one should make any assumptions about who will win the Trials, or about any prophecies that may or may not play out. Honestly, I just want to survive to see the end of the week." I rose to my feet and smiled. "I promise to help you all survive, too."

"Thanks," they replied in almost perfect unison.

With one last quick nod, I headed to the washroom to splash some cold water on my face. As I stared at myself in the mirror, I liked what I saw: A girl whose confidence was growing by the day. A girl who had survived several near-death experiences and was learning to fight for herself.

A girl who was beginning to like the idea of letting people in.

I TOOK A LONG SHOWER, put on my silver pajamas and headed to bed after a final goodnight to my new friends. I must have fallen asleep almost immediately, because the next thing I knew, Niala was shaking my shoulder gently.

"Vega, wake up," she was whispering. "Get dressed. The Headmaster wants to see you."

I opened my eyes to see a woman in gray standing at the foot of my bed, holding my linen clothing in her hands.

Without a word I leapt out of bed, changed into my clothes, and followed the woman out of the room, leaving the sleeping students behind. My heart was pounding, my mind turning over, questions swirling like a tornado.

Was I going to get kicked out? Had Merriwether found out about the time I was spending with Callum? Had something happened back at home?

No—that couldn't be it. Time at home was standing still.

But it had to be something. Merriwether wouldn't call me to his office in the middle of the night for nothing.

"Someone will collect your things," the woman said to me as we walked, which only cemented the notion that I was about to be expelled.

I nodded, too frightened to ask what was going on, and kept my mouth shut until we'd reached our destination.

"Vega," Merriwether said when he'd opened the door to his chamber. "Come, come." He ushered me inside, shutting the door behind me when my escort had left.

I trembled as I stepped inside the wood-paneled office, noting the incredible array of objects surrounding me. Everything from what looked like royal scepters to skulls to vials of dangerous-looking potion. The space glowed with light generated by a huge floating lantern hovering above an enormous wooden desk with the ornate carved legs of a lion.

"Sit down," Merriwether said, his voice low and even. I obeyed without question. After all, I was probably about to be sent home. What use would there be in protesting?

"Do you know why you're here?"

"No," I replied, determined to keep my answers monosyllabic to avoid giving away the tremor in my voice.

"Well, first of all," he said, "I owe you an apology."

Wait—the Headmaster of the Academy for the Blood-Born had gotten me out of bed to apologize...to...me?

"What?" I asked. "I mean pardon? I mean...what?"

"Freya's attack this afternoon was deliberate, calculated," he said, pacing behind his desk. "I should have known. I should have seen it coming."

"It's okay," I said.

"It's not okay, in fact, and it enrages me more than I care to say. It's not your fault the others see you as a threat, and it's unjust. Promise me now that you'll come to me if anyone else threatens you or makes you feel unsafe."

Okay…so maybe I wasn't being kicked out after all.

"I promise," I said. The words came out like a question. "Actually, they've been really nice since…the incident."

"Good, good. I'm glad to hear it. The most promising Seeker Candidate is always the least popular," Merriwether said, striding over and taking a seat in the leather chair on the opposite side of his enormous desk. "You were terrified, weren't you, when it happened?"

I stared at him, my heart pounding as I remembered the feeling of turning to swirling waves of smoke. The nothingness, the weightlessness that overtook my body. The feeling I'd become something else, something so far outside of myself that I was afraid I wouldn't be able to find my way back.

"Yes."

"Very few can do what you did," he said, an approving look in his eye. "Very few are what you are. But they do tend to be quite powerful."

"Powerful is a strange word for it," I said. "I felt like I'd…"

"Died?"

"Yes."

"It feels like death when one steps into the Shadow Realm," he said, as though he spoke from experience. "It's a horror, to be sure. I'm sorry I couldn't warn you in advance. The truth is, I had no way of knowing with any certainty you had it in you to become a Shadow."

"Warn me? Are you saying you had a suspicion I could do that?"

He half-shook, half-nodded his head. "Yes and no. I thought I detected something in those eyes of yours. They change color almost hourly now, which tells me that something inside you hasn't entirely settled on what you are."

"So I might have other...gifts?" I asked.

The word tasted bitter on my tongue. Summoning doors and losing myself in a cloud of purple smoke were quite enough for me.

Merriwether locked me in his gaze, his eyes twinkling under his unkempt brows. "I wish I could say with any certainty," he replied. "But I'm afraid I can't. You're quite different from anyone I've ever met."

Callum had said the same thing, but from him it was a compliment. From Merriwether it felt more like a curse. "Great," I puffed out. "With my luck, I'll probably grow spikes where my hands are and become some kind of dagger-fisted weirdo. Then the Zerkers will *really* have a reason to hate me."

"The Zerkers don't hate you, Vega."

He looked at the floor, and I watched as his hands tensed before relaxing again. "They're used to a certain routine around here. They're not accustomed to people wandering in from your world and showing themselves to be stronger, more powerful than they are. It frightens them, so they push back harder than they need to. It's a reflex, a survival instinct, like a wolf who growls when threatened."

I smiled to myself at the thought of scaring boys like Larken and Spiker.

"I don't mean to frighten anyone," I said. "I'm only here to help."

"I know." Merriwether picked up a book from his desk and leafed through it. "Listen, I need you to help me with something tonight—something dangerous and daunting. Are you up for it?"

"Everything is dangerous and daunting these days. Ever since my birthday. So what's one more challenge?"

"That's the spirit," Merriwether said with a wink. He spun around and strode over to press a glowing panel on the wall. A few seconds later the door opened and Niala walked through, with Rourke at her side in panther form.

I smiled when I saw the pair. If they were part of whatever the Headmaster was going to ask me to do, maybe I could come through it unscathed.

"There is a secret meeting set to take place at midnight," Merriwether said. "In a location few can reach. I need you to find your way there and to eavesdrop on the two people who are getting together. Then I need you to return and tell me what you've heard. Niala and Rourke will be on the lookout, ready to help you should you need it."

A strange smile crept over his features before he added, "Naturally, you'll need to use your newly-developed skill."

I nearly choked. "Wait—you mean my disappearing act?" I asked. "But...I have no idea how I even did that."

"A few days ago, you didn't know how to summon doors to other realms, yet here we are. I have no doubt when the time calls for it, you'll manage."

"But you saw us this morning—I'm terrible with weapons. I can't even—"

"I'm not sending you on an assassination mission, Vega. I'm sending you to listen. I suspect you're very good at that, although you're doing a terrible job at the moment."

I opened my mouth to protest again before stopping myself. Of course. This had to be another test to see if I was worthy of being named Seeker when all was said and done.

I had no choice but to do it.

"You're not to talk to anyone about what I'm going to show you," Merriwether said, looking at Niala and me in turn. "It is of the utmost importance that you keep quiet about this. Understood?"

We nodded in unison.

Merriwether opened the book he'd been leafing through and handed it to me. On a page on the right side was a painting of a cliff rising up out of the ocean, waves lapping at its base. A set of old ruins was perched high above at the top of the cliff, a heavy blanket of clouds hovering over the scene. Merriwether pointed to a black smear of paint at the base of the cliff that looked like a cavern of some sort.

"Do you think you can find your way to this place?" he asked.

I studied the painting for a minute before saying, "Maybe. But I don't even really know where we are right now."

"You didn't know where the Academy was, yet you managed to summon a door that led you to its library. You didn't know how to find the Otherwhere, yet you managed to summon the dragon's door into Anara."

"I think I get your point," I said with a sigh. "You want me to open a door to somewhere near that cave?"

"Yes. Two agents of the queen are meeting there in a few minutes. You need to find your way into the cave itself and wait for them to arrive. You, Vega, will hide inside while Niala and Rourke stand guard some distance away."

"Am I going to get a fancy black Ninja outfit to wear?" I asked.

"You won't need one. You're a Shadow, remember?"

I swallowed hard when the word met my ears. "But what if..."

"What if you can't disappear?" he asked. "If your power fails you?"

I nodded.

"It won't," he said simply.

When I opened my mouth to express doubt again, he held up a hand. "None of that," he said. "You know better."

I ground my jaw, reminding myself of Will's words just before we'd said good-bye to each other:

Don't be someone who sabotages herself on purpose to prove to the world how much you suck. You should be proving how amazing you are, because that's the real you.

I told myself that, no matter what happened tonight, I'd try to make my big brother proud.

I glanced over at Niala, who seemed to have already been briefed on the situation, because she looked far calmer than I felt.

"Okay, then," I said. "I guess it's a simple matter of opening a doorway to a super-dangerous place and going through, only to hope I can disappear into a swirling void when a couple of people who probably want to kill me show up?"

"That's about the size of it, yes," the Headmaster said with a smile. "Now you'd best get on with it. We don't have a lot of time."

Without another word, I nodded and looked at the painting once again. After I studied it for a minute, I closed my eyes and envisioned the sound of waves crashing against the shore, the smell of sea salt, the feeling of sand and stone beneath my feet.

When I opened my eyes, a door stood at the center of the chamber, a large wave carved into its surface. I rose to my feet, shot Niala and Rourke a quick, only slightly terrified smile, and unlocked the door.

A few seconds later, the three of us were standing on a rocky beach, angry waves crashing against the shore.

"I'll head up the path," Niala said, pointing to our right. A narrow trail led up to the sloping landscape above, where a series of large boulders offered a good hiding spot. "I'll send Rourke to let you know if we see anything threatening. You go stash yourself inside the cave. And be careful."

"You know," I said, "if someone had asked me to describe my perfect evening..."

"Yes?"

"This would be the opposite."

Niala threw me a grin. "The fact that the Headmaster assigned you this task is huge, you know. It shows that he trusts you more than anyone. You should be pleased."

"I would, if I had any confidence that I'd be alive in an hour."

"You will. By the way, I trust you to succeed. And so does Rourke. And Callum."

"I trust all of you, too. Now go stand guard so we don't all die horribly in some kind of fiery ambush, okay?"

"Done and done. Watch for a bird. He'll be your signal."

I nodded as Niala and her Familiar took off up the path. Then, I made my way along the shore until the cliff began cropping up in jagged, rocky shards to my right. As I walked, the terrain grew more inhospitable, and I had to navigate carefully to avoid breaking an ankle or flying into the water.

I got to the cavern after several minutes. Its opening was large, but the inside was shallower than I would have liked.

I'd just managed to stash myself at the back when I heard "Caw! Caw!" from a crow flying just outside the cave's mouth. No doubt it was Rourke's signal that I'd soon have company.

I swore under my breath as the faint glow from a lantern grew slowly brighter until the silhouette of a man appeared at the mouth of the cavern. Looking down at my hands, I could see they were shaking. Worse than that, they were still very definitely made of skin and bone.

Crap, crap, crap. How do I turn into a Shadow? I thought, trying to recall what had gone through my mind the moment it had happened in the sparring ring. But all I could remember was fear. Fear for my life, fear that my head was about to get crushed in. Fear I'd never see Will, Liv, or Callum again.

When the man with the lantern spun around and the light fell in beams against the cave walls, that same fear assaulted me. I could see his face now—a set of angry, bright eyes glowing crimson in the darkness. Stringy hair that looked like it had never encountered shampoo. At his waist was a long dagger that had probably slit more than a few throats in its time. The guy made Freya look like a plush doll.

I cowered, knowing full well that if he saw me, I was dead. Niala and Rourke were too far away to help now, and I was on my own. But the man turned around once again, grumbling something about his colleague being late.

As I watched him, I felt the same horrible emptiness that had assaulted me earlier, like everything that made me whole was dissipating, torn away by my own terror. I looked down once again to see the fear had turned me all but invisible for the second time in a day. My fingers trailed into the air in wisps of dark smoke, unfocused and inexplicably bizarre.

As my fear began to ebb, I found myself able to hold onto my Shadow form. As with the summoning of the doors, I was learning to control this power.

With my confidence growing, I managed to slip along the cave's wall until I was closer to the mouth, close enough to hear even the quietest conversation. After a few seconds I was near enough to the man to reach out and touch him, and the thought of it filled me with a feeling of power I'd never known before. I was beginning to understand how Shadows had become assassins over the centuries, sneaking up on unsuspecting victims and slitting their throats from behind.

After a minute or so, the second person arrived.

I recognized her immediately. A tall woman with white-blond hair, the Waerg who had dug her way inside my mind on the street in Fairhaven.

I could only hope she couldn't detect my presence now.

"Took you long enough," the man snarled as she came close.

"I like to be fashionably late, Barnabas. You know that," she said.

"Yeah, well, the tide's going to rise, and we'll drown if you don't spit out whatever it is you want to tell me, and soon."

I looked outside, panicked. He was right—the waves had

begun lapping higher and higher, and now threatened to make their way inside the cave. And something told me that being in Shadow form wouldn't save me from drowning.

"You first," the woman said.

The man let out an exasperated breath. "Fine. Rumor has it that the girl—the one you tried to grab and failed due to your utter incompeten—"

"Watch yourself, Barney. You don't want me walking into that shriveled husk you call a brain and pulling out all your secrets, do you?"

"It's just that…the Sloane girl—"

I stifled a gasp at hearing my name. These people, these awful creatures, were meeting to talk about…me.

"What about her?" the woman asked, clearly annoyed.

"They say she's a Shadow."

The woman froze for a moment, then let out a high-pitched, highly amused laugh.

"What's so damned funny?" the man asked.

"She's not a Shadow. She's a damned Summoner," the woman said. "I watched her do it. I watched her open a Breach, for God's sake."

"So?"

"So, a Summoner can't also be a Shadow."

"My source tells me she did it this afternoon at the Academy. Saved her life, too."

"Not possible," the woman reiterated with a dismissive snarl and a gnashing of her teeth.

The man held up his hands in surrender. "Okay, okay," he said. "Fine. You would know. Just tell me what you have, and let's be done with it."

"The Mistress," she said, "has acquired five dragons. She intends to tame them."

"Pfft," Barnabas scoffed. "No one's managed that in centuries. Dragons are feral monsters, at best."

"She's also acquired something else. Something…magnificent."

"More magnificent than Dragons?"

The woman shot him an angry look.

"I'm no fan of theirs," the man said. "But you must concede that they are handsome creatures."

"I don't have to concede anything," she said. "And yes—what she has acquired is more magnificent than Dragons. It's something that will put an end to this nonsense with the Sloane girl and stop her dead."

"And you're sure about this?"

"I've seen it."

"But that means…" He was speaking softly now, barely more than a whisper. I edged closer, hoping to make out what he was saying. But before Barnabas could finish his thought, a sound erupted nearby—the unmistakable timbre of men's voices.

"Damn it, the night guard is on the prowl," he said with an upward flick of his head. "They're on the cliff's edge up above us. Come on, we need to get back before they see us."

With that, the two of them took off, the light from the lantern fading fast behind them as I was left alone at the mouth of the cave.

I looked down to see in the faint moonlight that my skin was still swirling with purple smoke, as were my clothes. I rose to my feet and skulked out of the cave, making my way along the shore once again, my eyes peeled for Niala and Rourke.

After a few minutes I breathed a sigh of relief as I heard the reassuring sound of a crow circling overhead. I lifted my head to see Niala jogging down the path toward me.

"Vega! Are you there? They've gone!" she whispered. It took me a moment to realize she was looking around, searching for me. Of course—she still couldn't see me.

I closed my eyes, willing myself visible, and in an instant, I was back in my solid form. A wave of nausea overtook me, and I had to reach for Niala's arm to steady myself.

"You all right?" she asked.

"I will be. It feels like everything's moving around...like my body's still figuring out how it works. But I'll be okay."

"Did you find anything out?"

"A few things," I replied with a nod. "None of them good."

THE TOWER

"TELL ME," MERRIWETHER SAID, POURING A GLASS OF ICE WATER and handing it my way as I threw myself into the leather chair in his office. I hadn't realized how exhausted I was until that minute, but it seemed the Headmaster had expected it. "Summoning on top of Shadow-casting has taken a lot out of you," he added. "Take your time."

I took the water gratefully, chugging the entire glass before speaking. I went on to tell him and Niala what I'd heard about the dragons the Usurper Queen had acquired.

"Dragons," Merriwether said. "That could be very bad indeed. Then again, they're as likely to try to kill the queen as not. Perhaps they could do our job for us." He eyed me for a moment. "There's something else," he said. "Go on."

I swallowed hard before speaking. "They mentioned me by name," I said. "More than once."

"What did they say?"

"The man...Barnabas...he said he heard I'm a Shadow."

Merriwether and Niala exchanged a horrified look. "You know what this means," Merriwether said. Niala nodded.

"Wait—what does it mean?" I asked.

"It means," Merriwether drawled, as if reluctant to say the words out loud, "that we have a spy among us."

"Worse than a spy," Niala said, a quiver in her voice. "A traitor."

I slouched down in my chair. "Look. I just got here. You know these people, I don't. You recruited them. And there are plenty who don't seem to like me too much. Can't you just put them in a room somewhere under some hot lights until someone confesses? What about that Freya girl? The others don't think she hates me, but she *did* try to kill me..."

"It would be the obvious answer," Merriwether agreed. "But I don't think so. I have it on good authority she was escorted home by two of our Rangers. She's no longer in the Otherwhere."

"Where is she?"

Merriwether paused, drumming his fingers on his desk.

"Actually, she's been expelled for what she did in your sparring session."

"So she really was—?"

"Trying to kill you?" Merriwether shrugged. "Whether she was or not, we couldn't take a chance letting her stay after her little stunt. The faculty agreed things could only get worse from there. If she did want you dead, she'd keep trying until she succeeded. So we took action to ensure your safety."

I thought about this for a second. "Still, once she got escorted out of the Otherwhere, she could have made a bee-line to Barnabas and told him all about me."

"Not possible," Merriwether said. "Even if she wanted to, Seeker Candidates can't go through portals unaccompanied. With your door-summoning ability, you're the only one who can pass back and forth on your own."

I raised an eyebrow, surprised at this new information.

"I told you," Merriwether said, "you're more powerful than you realize."

"So if it's not Freya..."

"It's someone else," Niala finished. "Someone who is still here at the Academy."

Merriwether looked troubled, which unsettled me more than I wanted to admit. I tried to think of every student who'd been in the courtyard today, but I couldn't imagine who would have been able to get word to the man called Barnabas.

"I'll be speaking to the other instructors about this," Merriwether promised. "Perhaps one of them has some thoughts."

"There's something else," I blurted out. "The woman—the Waerg who was at the meeting—she said the queen had acquired something that would stop me dead."

"Did she say what?" Merriwether asked, his eyebrows arched high. "Did she mention a Relic of Power?"

I shook my head. "No. Not that I heard, anyway. Before they could discuss it, they heard men approaching and stopped talking."

"Then we'll have to keep an eye out. But don't worry, Vega—nothing can come through the Academy's doors uninvited."

"That's reassuring," I said, and for once, I meant it.

"In the meantime, you need to steer clear of the dormitory tonight."

He rose to his feet and hit the button on the wall next to the bookshelf, and a moment later, a woman dressed in a gray suit waltzed into the room.

"Come with me," she said, signaling me to join her.

After Merriwether nodded his assent, I followed her without a word, only to find myself being led down a series of corridors and up a narrow spiral staircase at the center of a cylindrical tower.

"Where are we going?" I asked.

"Private quarters," she replied. "Headmaster wants you isolated from the other Candidates for your own safety."

I was about to ask why, but it would have been a seriously stupid question. Someone had told the enemy about my powers.

That same person would probably be rewarded if they put a knife in my chest.

A minute later, we reached a level at the top of the tower, where four doors greeted us.

"Sloane, you take number three. Room number four is the bathroom."

"Who's in the other two?" I asked.

"Mr. Drake and Lady Gray."

My heart leapt to learn that Callum would be sleeping so close by. I eyed doors one and two, wondering which one he was behind, but when I caught the woman in gray giving me a judgmental look, I shook off my daydream, thanked her, and made my way into room number three.

The room was small but quaintly apportioned, with a window looking out toward the moon hovering over the sea. A small white bed sat against one wall, a nightstand at its side. By some miracle, my gear was all there, my clothing hung carefully in a narrow, open wardrobe to one side of the window.

After about five minutes of settling in, someone knocked at my door. I opened it, expecting to see the woman in gray on the other side. But it was Callum who greeted me.

"Hello, neighbor," he said cheerfully. "Can I come in?"

"Into my room?" I asked. I'd never had a boy in my room back home, and the thought of it sent a shudder of excitement through me. *Whoa. What would Liv say if she could see me now?*

"Well, yes," Callum said with a chuckle. "Into your room."

"Of course."

I gestured for him to come in, and I closed the door behind him.

"I just wanted to make sure you're okay," he said.

"You know why I'm up here, then?"

He nodded. "Well, I can guess. Merriwether told me earlier he was sending you on a mission."

"It seems someone's out for my blood. Other than Freya, I mean. The Headmaster says I'm not safe."

"I told you," he said with a sigh. "You're an amazing freak. That makes you an automatic target."

"At the moment, I don't feel the least bit amazing."

Callum stepped forward and wrapped his arms around me, which surprised me, but I was grateful for the gesture. I turned my head to the side, unsure whether to laugh or cry.

"What do I do?" I asked, my voice vibrating against his chest.

"You go about your business. You hone your skills. You continue to prove yourself. It's more important than ever that you're the selected Seeker when the time comes."

"*If* the time comes. At this rate, I'm going to get killed before the Trials even start."

"I won't let that happen," he said, pulling away.

"It's not your job to protect me, Callum."

"I know. But I want to, if I can. I want to make sure you have a chance at the best life you can have. I know how strong you are—but until *you* know, I'll stick around to keep an eye on you."

I smiled up at him through damp eyes. "How do you always say the right thing?" I asked. "I freak out about certain death, then you come along and calm me right down."

He shot me a serious look. "Vega, you're not just important to me because of your crazy-powerful magical abilities, you know. I told you ages ago, you're unlike anyone I've ever met. I care about you."

"You do?"

He nodded, and I realized for the first time that his face was so near mine that I could feel his breath on my skin.

"I do," he said, pressing his lips gently to mine.

I'd craved this moment since the first time I'd set eyes on him. I'd ached for the sensation that was hitting me now.

I felt myself growing light once again, floating above the ground. But this time it wasn't because I was disappearing. This was the very opposite. For the first time in years, the void inside me was beginning to fill. I was becoming whole again.

Callum eased away and looked at me, stroking a finger over my right cheekbone. "I've got to say," he murmured, "I don't really see you needing my help. You're pretty kick-arse on your own, you know."

"Kick-*arse*?" I asked with a snicker. "You're so bloody English."

"Fine," he said, a rumbling chuckle building in his chest. "Kick-ass, then." The word came out with some sort of mock-American twang.

"Oh, God no," I chortled. "Stick to your own accent. It's much sexier."

"Sexy, is it?" he asked with a raised eyebrow. "Vega Sloane thinks I'm sexy, does she?"

"Great. Now I've done it," I said, rolling my eyes. "You're going to be intolerable now that you know, aren't you?"

"Maybe."

His lips met mine again, and this time I was ready for it. I found myself pushing my fingers into his mane of thick hair, blood pulsing through my veins in a torrent that exhilarated me more than fear of death ever could. The kiss lasted a long time, yet not long enough, the taste of his tongue lingering on my own. I felt like the whole tower was swaying, ready to collapse from the force of our connection.

But I didn't mind one bit.

"Stay with me," I said when we'd pulled apart.

"I don't know. It's sort of against the rules..." Callum said, eyeing my narrow bed.

"My grandmother was a rule-breaker. It's in my blood. Stay with me."

I took him by the hand and, walking backwards, led him with me until the backs of my legs were touching the mattress. "Besides, if I'm going to live in constant danger, surely I deserve one nice experience. Don't I?"

"Can't argue with that," Callum said with a crooked, mischievous smile.

"It will be the most innocent night in history. I promise."

After giving him a peck on the cheek, I lay down on the bed. Callum eased in behind me, his arm around my waist, and within seconds I was asleep.

It was the best night of my life.

THE PIT

THE FOLLOWING MORNING AT BREAKFAST, A PROJECTION OF Merriwether's face appeared over our tables and told the twelve remaining Seeker Candidates to meet in a small courtyard at the Academy's northern end for another round of sparring.

"The session will be closed this time," Merriwether explained. "And it will be conducted quite differently from yesterday's."

Other than that, he told us nothing whatsoever about what we were up against.

I wondered why we weren't starting the day with more weapons training. I couldn't speak for anyone else, but when it came to weapons, one day was hardly enough.

But Merriwether always had his reasons, so I kept my mouth shut and headed to the courtyard with the others.

"You will be fighting against one of our instructors," Merriwether announced in person when we arrived, gesturing toward a young woman I'd seen on the stage at the Assembly on my first day. She'd looked familiar then, though I hadn't quite been able to figure out why.

"Miss Carlaw is a shape-shifter. She will be making use of her skill in an attempt to throw you off your game."

Of course—that was why I had the feeling I'd seen her before. She was a shifter, like the Waergs I'd been unfortunate enough to encounter in Fairhaven. Fortunately, Miss Carlaw didn't give off the same evil vibe that they had. Her face was kind, thoughtful. Almost angelic.

Though I had little doubt that she was planning to put us through our paces.

Merriwether looked at each of us before continuing. "You may use any skills at your disposal. Just please don't get carried away, and Miss Carlaw has promised me she'll return the favor. Your job is to prove yourselves able to immobilize her. I want to see what you're made of."

With that, the Headmaster told us to step back to the perimeter of the courtyard. When we'd done so, he made a sweeping gesture with his right hand toward the center of the dirt floor, which swirled open until a broad, circular, flat-bottomed pit stood in front of us.

"You will fight inside the pit," he said. "For most of you there is no escape, of course, so evasion probably won't be an option. You'll have to use your wits, your strength, and any other weapons and skills at your disposal."

"Except for *actual* weapons," said Callum, who stepped up to stand next to Merriwether. As I stared at him, memories of last night flooded my mind in pleasant waves, which I told myself to push away until later. Getting distracted by my feelings for Callum wasn't exactly going to hand me an advantage in a one-on-one battle with an experienced instructor.

I eyed the pit with more confidence than I'd had on my first two days at the Academy. I told myself I had a definite advantage: I would be able to summon a Breach and escape—and if that didn't work, I could turn to Shadow and buy myself some time until I figured out a way to take Miss Carlaw down.

The first Candidate Merriwether called upon was Meg, who looked supremely terrified as she slipped down into the pit, which must have been an eight-foot drop at least. We stepped carefully to the edge to watch as Miss Carlaw slid down opposite her, immediately shifting into a sleek tiger.

"Oh, man," I heard someone say to my right. "Meg's toast."

Meg and the tiger began to circle each other, with Meg looking scared to death as she felt her way along the dirt wall. She shut her eyes, trying to summon her power, but to no avail. I'd heard her telling one of the other students she could move exceedingly fast in short bursts, which sometimes helped her to surprise her opponents. But I had yet to see her pull that particular little gimmick out of her bag of tricks.

The tiger lunged at her a few times and swiped at the air in front of her face but was careful never to make actual contact. Meg cowered against the wall, her lower lip trembling.

"Come on, Meg!" I yelled. I supposed it wasn't the smartest thing to root for my competition, but I couldn't stand watching her give up. "Remember what you can do!"

She shot me a grateful look, narrowed her eyes, and zipped at lightning-speed across the circular hole in the ground. The tiger, confused, spun around, but Meg had already come up behind her, leaping in a single motion onto the creature's back and throwing her arms in a hammer-lock around the big cat's neck.

The tiger morphed back into Miss Carlaw, who rose to her feet to congratulate the Candidate. "Well done," she said, rubbing her neck. "That was an excellent start."

Callum lowered a rope ladder for a beaming Meg to climb out.

Then the next Candidate went in, then another, and another.

The test turned out to be a good one, challenging each participant to come up with creative solutions to the dilemma of being trapped in a deep hole with an angry carnivore. The boy with the rosy cheeks and dark hair turned out to be a Digger who managed to accurately predict the tiger's every move and avoid her attacks until the beast tired herself out and needed a break.

Oleana, who turned out to be a Chiller—a caster who could summon frost projectiles—lost her fight marginally by misinterpreting one of the tiger's leaps and getting her spell off too late. The tiger pinned her up against the wall, teeth bared, before backing down and leaving Oleana to ponder her mistake.

By the time it was my turn, I was worried that Miss Carlaw must be exhausted. I leapt down into the pit and asked, "Do you need another break? Some water?"

She shot me a look of thanks and said, "I'm fine. Just go easy on me, okay?"

With a smile, I nodded. "I'll do my best."

I'd watched Candidate after Candidate use their magical skills against the tiger, studied her moves, and for once I felt entirely confident I would come out of this session triumphant.

But first, in a moment of cockiness, I decided to show off a bit.

After Miss Carlaw shifted, I began to circle the ring, watching the tiger pad around, her mouth slightly open as she fixed her amber eyes on me.

"You can see me now," I said softly, a challenging grin on my face. "I'm sure I look like a tasty snack to you. But that won't last long."

With that, I slammed my eyes shut and asked the Shadow to come, for my body to vanish, overtaken by nebulous vapor.

But when I opened my eyes and looked down, nothing had happened. I stared at my hands, panicked. Had I lost my skill? Had I been too confident, too arrogant?

Maybe I wasn't frightened enough to disappear.

"Oh, no," I muttered.

Even the tiger looked puzzled, as if she knew what I'd just tried to do.

I began circling the pit faster. My only option now was to open a Breach. I'd summon a door into the Grove, use the dragon key to open it, and slip through. I'd summoned enough doors by now to know I could do it anytime, anywhere, and quickly.

I reached for the dragon key and tore it off its chain, ready to lunge through the door the second it appeared.

But once again, when I pictured the orange tree at the Grove's center and called forth the door, nothing happened.

I could feel my eyes popping open wide as more panic set in.

The tiger advanced, the muscles in its shoulders and hind legs twitching in preparation for a lunge. The black claws extended out and down, curving into the ground.

"What are you doing, Vega?" someone above yelled. "Do something!"

"I can't!" I shouted back. "I've been…shut down, or something."

I looked up to see Callum and Merriwether standing side by side at the edge of the pit. Their faces were mostly in shadow, but I could see they both looked deeply concerned.

I darted around the pit, keeping as far from the tiger as I could, knowing I had no natural defenses against it. If Miss Carlaw decided not to play nice, I could easily end up in the infirmary.

My back to the far wall, I tried again to call upon my powers, but each time I was met with a wall of weakness.

I stared at the tiger's slit-pupiled eyes. "I understand what you have to do," I said, "so maybe you should just get it over with."

As if in response, the tiger leapt at me once again, hurtling its large body through the air in front of me. I braced myself, thrusting my hands out in front of my face and wincing as I awaited the painful moment of impact.

But it never came.

The tiger seemed to freeze in mid-air, its body going rigid. She fell to the ground, eyes open.

It took me a moment to see that something large was protruding from her side—a dart?

Wait—had Merriwether tranquilized her?

"You didn't have to do that!" I shouted. "She was about to win, fair and—"

"What are those things?" someone yelled.

I looked up, my pulse racing, to see a series of metallic, winged objects, each about the size and shape of a large hawk, hovering over the courtyard. At first there were only four or five, but they were quickly joined by what seemed like hundreds.

"What's happening?" I shouted.

"Hunter Drones!" I heard Callum yell. "Everyone, get back!"

He raced around and dropped the ladder down for me, but even as I reached it, a series of large darts pierced the earth at my feet. I jerked my head up to see his eyes staring frantically down at me. Once again, he pulled his gaze upward, only to see another barrage of projectiles flying down toward the pit.

"Stay against the wall, Vega!" Callum yelled, positioning himself directly above me. "Don't move!"

"But they'll kill you!" I shouted.

"No, they won't!"

Without another word, he leapt into the air. I couldn't understand what he was doing or why. For a second it looked like he was going to belly-flop into the pit. But as he soared out over the large hole in the ground, darkness engulfed me from above, as though a protective ceiling had formed above Miss Carlaw and me.

A moment later, the "ceiling" began to rise up, higher and higher, until it narrowed to a long series of golden scales. All of a sudden, a vast set of exquisite wings was beating at the sky above me.

The ceiling, it turned out, was no ceiling.

I was staring at the glistening, chain-mail underside of a golden dragon.

DANGER

I WATCHED THE FLYING CREATURE SLICE AND BANK THROUGH THE sky, and I stared, open-mouthed, as it shot spikes of flame at every drone along the way. Too confused to think straight, I raced over to Miss Carlaw, who was lying paralyzed on the ground at the center of the pit. Within seconds, Merriwether had jumped down into the pit and was at my side, his hand on her neck as he hunted for a pulse.

"She's alive," he said. "Barely. We need to get her some help. Are you all right, Vega?"

I nodded. "I am, thanks to..." I pulled my eyes up to the sky.

"The drones kept you from casting. The queen must have done something to them—added a charm, or a spell of some sort. They kept my magic at bay, too. This must be the secret weapon you heard about last night. It's a lucky thing that shape-shifting isn't a suppressible talent, or things could have been much worse."

I nodded, my eyes shooting upwards once again. The dragon was now circling overhead, fire shooting from its mouth as it scorched the last of the drones to piles of flitting ash in the sky.

"Is that..." I began.

"You're wondering if the dragon you're looking at is our very own Mr. Drake," Merriwether said. "And the answer is yes."

"He's really a Dragon shifter? Like the Crimson King?"

"He is," Merriwether said. "Though he was trying his best to keep his gift a secret, for what should seem like obvious reasons. Now come, climb out of here, and run and tell the others that I could use some help down here with Miss Carlaw."

I nodded and raced to the rope ladder, climbing out as fast as I could.

"Get help," I told Meg and the others, who ran inside to search for the nearest faculty members.

My eyes searched the sky again, seeing nothing now but blue. Callum—the Dragon version of himself, anyhow—had disappeared from view. But, fortunately, so had the drones.

As soon as a few faculty members came running out to help Merriwether lift Miss Carlaw and carry her to the infirmary, I sprinted to the nearest bathroom, called up a Breach, and made my way into the Grove. Something told me that if Callum was to be found anywhere, it would be there. I was desperate to talk to him, to find out if he was okay.

I found him sitting on the grass at the Grove's center, his legs tucked up under his chin. He looked tense, his arms wrapped around his shins, eyes focused on a spot on the ground in front of him. The look on his face was one I'd never seen before. He looked…tortured.

"You nearly died," he said softly as I approached.

"But I didn't," I replied, sitting down next to him. "Thanks to you."

He shot me a quick look before pulling his eyes away. "I took too long to react. I waited too long, all because I didn't want…"

"Because you didn't want everyone knowing who you are? That seems perfectly reasonable, actually. Word spreads fast around here, and it seems like no one can be trusted."

"It doesn't matter. I'm so sorry, Vega. I wish I could've told you sooner. I wish I hadn't kept such a huge secret from you."

"That you're the heir to the throne, you mean?" I asked.

He winced his eyes shut and nodded.

"So it's true. You're the descendant of the Crimson King. Like in the prophecy."

He nodded again. "I didn't want anyone thinking my agenda was to win the throne. That's not why the Academy exists. That's not why we need to fight the queen. I don't care about taking charge. I never have. All I want is for the Otherwhere to stay peaceful and beautiful, as it's always been. I don't want my home corrupted by ambition and cruelty."

"Huh. That sounds like something a really good king might say."

A crooked smile slipped over Callum's lips as he turned my way, picking a piece of grass out of the ground and peeling it apart. "You're really not freaked out by what you saw?" he asked.

"That you just turned into a huge fire-breathing beast who could barbecue me in seconds?" I replied with a shrug and a smirk. "No. Actually, it explains a thing or two. Besides, I turn into a smoke monster who calls forth doors to really weird places, so I'd say I almost have you beat."

"Well, the cat's out of the bag now, I suppose. Speaking of cats, is Miss Carlaw going to be okay?"

"I don't know," I said, my smile fading. "I hope so. But those darts…they were meant for me, weren't they?"

Callum nodded slowly. "I'm afraid so. The queen obviously sees you as a serious threat."

"I thought she couldn't reach us at the Academy. I thought we were safe here. Merriwether said—"

"We are safe—for the most part. But it would seem the sky is out of Merriwether's reach. He can only cast so many protective spells. If I'd known what they were going to do, I'd never have suggested we use the courtyards."

"You couldn't have known the queen would send those drones. None of us could have. But now we do. She's wanted me dead for ages, and today she nearly got her wish."

"Perhaps not dead after all," a deep voice said from somewhere behind us, causing us both to jump. Callum and I twisted around to see Merriwether standing on the grass between two trees, a grave look on his face. "Those darts weren't meant to kill. Only to get your attention. They were laced with a paralyzing poison. Painful, but it fades in a few hours."

"So Miss Carlaw will be all right?" I asked.

"Yes. She'll be fine."

"Thank God." I rose to my feet and faced him.

He didn't look as relieved as I'd hoped.

"What's wrong?" I asked.

Callum pushed himself up to stand next to me, attentively waiting for the answer to my question.

"Come with me. Both of you," Merriwether said. "There's something I need to show you."

Once we were inside, Merriwether led us down a series of halls until we came to his office, where he shut the door and locked it behind us.

"Sit down, Miss Sloane, Mr. Drake," he said as he stepped over to his desk and took a seat. "What I have to tell you is of the gravest importance and needs to be kept secret in order to avoid mass panic. Is that understood?"

Callum and I exchanged a look and nodded our heads. "Understood," we said.

Merriwether reached under his desk and pulled up an object I'd seen before in the Academy's library: a sphere swirling with purple.

The *Orb of Kilarin*, he'd called it.

The last time I'd seen it, it had been flickering with the image of a grim-looking castle at its center. Now, I couldn't entirely make out what the image was, other than a couple of oddly moving shadows.

"While the drones were attacking, a message came to me via the orb," the Headmaster said, sweeping a hand over the sphere. "Sent from the Usurper Queen."

As he pulled his hand away, the image became clearer. Inside the orb was the image of two silhouettes floating in a swirling green liquid. They looked like a boy and a girl, each of their bodies suspended helplessly inside a large cylindrical tank. I leaned in to look more closely, but even as I did so, I could feel Callum's hand reaching for my arm as if in warning.

His grip tightened.

"What is it?" I asked. "What am I seeing?"

A moment later, the answer came to me as a tsunami of nausea swept through my insides.

Will...

Liv...

Floating suspended somewhere, unconscious, unmoving.

Prisoners.

"Where are they?" I asked, my voice rising with panic. "What's happened to them?"

"She's taken them," Merriwether said. "The Usurper Queen has taken them as a means to persuade you to leave the Academy and to forfeit the Trials."

"How do you know?" I asked. "I mean, how do we know this isn't just some trick of hers?"

Merriwether sat back and turned his attention to the far wall, where a screen sprang to life and a letter, handwritten, began to scroll across its surface.

"Vega Sloane," it read, "must willingly surrender the Dragon Key to my agents. She must then return to Fairhaven, never to return to the Otherwhere. If my demands are not met, her brother and her friend will die."

"The signature is marked with her official seal," he said, pointing out a swirling design in the lower right corner.

A choking sob made its way up to my throat. Callum's hand was still on my arm, and I reached for it, digging my fingertips into his skin as I looked for comfort. But he wasn't enough to protect me. Not this time. Not from this.

My brother and my best friend would both die if I didn't meet the queen's demands.

"We have to save them!" I shouted. "We have to get them away from her!"

"They're in her castle," Merriwether said. "And I'm afraid it's not exactly the sort of place you can just wander up to. She has an army of thousands of Waergs. They prowl the woods all around the palace. And if Mr. Drake flew up in dragon form, they'd see him coming from ten miles away."

I took a deep breath, telling myself to calm down, that freaking out wasn't going to help anyone or anything.

"So what do you suggest?" I asked, shooting a look at the orb. I stared at the floating image of Liv and Will, who seemed to be suspended in giant glass tubes in the middle of a room of stone. Carved dragons perched like gargoyles above them, guardians seemingly put in place to ensure they couldn't escape.

"We have two options," Merriwether said. "One is you do as she asks—which would put the Otherwhere at risk, because it would mean losing our most promising Candidate."

"There are eleven other Candidates chomping at the bit to be the chosen Seeker. Why is she so worried about me? Surely it can't all be because there's some prophecy making the rounds."

"She's worried because she knows who you truly are," Merriwether said. "She knows where you come from. She knows who your grandfather really was."

"*I* don't even know who my grandfather was," I said miserably. I pulled my eyes to Callum's for a moment before saying, "Well, it doesn't even matter, not anymore. I have no choice. I'll have to drop out of the Academy. Anything else would be selfish."

Merriwether looked pensive. "Your decision is, of course, yours to make. Might I suggest, though, that you sleep on it for one night before turning the key in? You may find that morning brings a change of heart."

"You think I'll be able to sleep while some nutjob of a queen tortures my brother and my best friend?"

"At the risk of sounding cold, they don't feel anything, Vega. They don't know she's taken them. And the Usurper Queen won't do anything to them while she knows she can use them as leverage. You have the luxury of a little time. You mustn't rush into a decision that could alter the course of your entire life."

I inhaled deep, fighting off the desire to scream. "You're right," I said, my voice strained as I rose to my feet. "I'm sorry—this has been a lot to digest. I'm going to head to my room and lie down, if it's all right. I need to think."

"That is a very good plan."

Without another word, I made my way to the tower where my room and Callum's were located and climbed the narrow, dizzyingly tall spiral staircase until I arrived at our floor.

Once inside my room, I perched on the edge of my bed, my face in my hands. It felt like years had passed since my seventeenth birthday. Years since I'd awoken to find my Nana's card. Years since I'd hugged Will goodbye and told him I loved him.

Now he and Liv were prisoners of the Mistress. The awful woman who'd stolen Callum's rightful place on the throne, who wanted to destroy this beautiful land and to ransack my world along with it. Will and Liv were puppets inside her grim castle. And unless someone did what she asked, they'd never be set free. I'd go home, which meant I'd never see Merriwether or Niala again, or the pristine fields of Anara.

Worst of all, I'd never see Callum again.

As I pondered the wretched thought, a knock sounded at my door.

"Come in," I moaned.

"You okay?" Callum asked as he pushed the door open and stepped inside.

"No," I replied. "I'm so far from okay that I'd need a passport to *get* to okay."

He frowned and walked over to sit on the edge of the bed next to me, putting an arm around my shoulder.

"I just wanted a chance," I said. "I wanted to prove to myself I could succeed. That I was worth something. That my parents didn't die in vain. I wanted to beat the woman who destroyed my family. But now she's beaten me. She's taken everything from me."

"You don't have to prove anything to anyone, Vega. You are worth everything. As for the queen, she doesn't matter. She's cruel and manipulative. She's trying to break you, but she doesn't know how strong you really are. Don't worry—we'll get Will and Liv back."

"Maybe I'm not strong at all," I said, wiping a tear away from my cheek and turning to look into his eyes. "Maybe I'm too weak for…"

A sudden thought surged like wildfire through my mind. My spine straightened and I curled my fingers around the edge of the mattress.

"What is it?" asked Callum, who'd noticed the shift in my demeanor.

"He never said what the second option was."

"What?"

"Merriwether said there were two options. The first was to return to Fairhaven. But he never named the second. Does that seem like the kind of mistake a man like him would make?"

Callum thought about it for a few seconds before shaking his head.

With a smile, I turned his way, pressed a palm to his cheek, and kissed him. "I need to go," I said, pulling myself to my feet. "There's someone I need to see."

"Vega..." Callum began, leaping to his feet. "You can't take on the queen yourself."

"Maybe I can, maybe I can't," I replied, slamming my eyes shut. "But I'm not *going* to see her. Not yet, anyhow."

"Then who...?"

"Someone who can give me the answers I need," I said, opening my eyes again to see the door I'd summoned standing in front of me.

"I'm not sure this is such a good idea," Callum said, thrusting himself between the door and me. "Whatever you're intending to do, you should think about it first. If you leave this place—"

"If I leave, then what? I'll be kicked out of the Academy? I won't be able to compete in the Trials?" I said with a bitter laugh. "I'll never see you again? All those things are already becoming reality. But maybe if I can get my answers, I can figure out a way to save Will and Liv, and to find my way back to you."

Throwing his hands in the air in surrender, Callum stepped aside.

I reached for the dragon key, tore it from its chain, and shot him a final look. "You told me last night that you care about me. I need you to know that I care about you, too. So much that it hurts."

I pushed myself up onto my tiptoes, kissed him one last time, and a second later, I was gone.

THROUGH THE DOOR

THE SMELL OF SEAWEED MET MY NOSE AS I STEPPED THROUGH TO the other side. Long, brownish grass swept across the ground, tickling my legs, and a familiar sense of calm filled me, replacing the anger and despair I'd felt only a moment ago.

In front of me stood a little stone cottage, a series of colorful potted plants hanging from its porch roof.

Despite everything that had happened, a smile worked its way over my lips. Seeing the cottage was like a homecoming. It was familiar, comforting. And, best of all, the woman inside might help me to save Will and Liv.

I strode forward until I came to the door, but before I had a chance to knock, it opened inward to reveal a small, white-haired woman staring me in the face.

"I was expecting you, Vega dear," she said. "Though perhaps not this soon."

"Nana," I said, a sob forming in my throat as I threw my arms around her.

"It's all right," she replied, patting my back. "Come in for some tea, and tell me what's happened."

I followed her in and sat down at the kitchen table while she put the kettle on. In my haste to fill her in, it took me all of two minutes to explain what had happened—my turning into a Shadow, the drones, the abduction. The only part I didn't tell her about was Callum.

"So, the Usurper Queen knows what you are," my grandmother said, turning to me with a raised eyebrow. "She's right to be frightened of you, you know."

"Frightened of me? What, because I can call up doors and turn into smoke?"

Nana shook her head. "You can do so much more than that," she said. "You just don't know it yet."

I narrowed my eyes and chewed my lip for a moment. The question was hard to ask, but at this point, I had no other choice.

"Nana—who is my grandfather?"

My grandmother pressed her hands onto the counter and leaned back, rocking on her heels. "It's so strange," she said. "I've known for years that this question would come. Your father never knew that the man who raised him was a stepfather, of course. Never suspected a thing. As far as he was concerned, the fisherman he knew so well was his flesh and blood."

"But he wasn't, of course," I said.

Nana shook her head. "No." When the kettle began whistling, she spun around and turned the heat off. "When I was a little older than you," she said, twisting back around, "I fell madly in love with a very gifted young man."

"That was the scandal. The one they talk about at the Academy."

"They still talk about it, do they? Bunch of gossips." She let out a chuckle. "I suppose it shouldn't be surprising. They all think I ran off with a Waerg, or worse. It's very exciting to them, I'm sure, to think I might have carried the enemy's baby."

"Didn't you?"

"Of course not," Nana said, flapping a tea towel in my direction like she was swatting at a fly. "I only told them I did. You see, the man I loved was someone important, and I knew it. When I discovered I was going to have his child, I knew if I allowed his reputation to be ruined, I would be destroying all his potential in one go. I couldn't do that, so naturally, I made up a story about falling for the enemy. I protected him and returned to Cornwall in shame. But I didn't care. I received the most wonderful gift in the end. I got your father in the bargain."

"Who…who was the man? I really need to know."

"He was the most handsome creature. And so skilled in the ways of magic. He was the best the Academy had ever seen. In fact, they didn't know how to classify him—red, blue, green—so they gave him his own color."

I was about to ask what she meant when my mouth dropped open.

"Purple," I breathed.

"Purple," she echoed. "Purple for the wizard who turned to shadow when called upon. The wizard who could summon protective spells, who could make flowers grow on stone. The wizard who would one day run the Academy for the Blood-Born."

"Merriwether…is my grandfather?" I gasped.

He'd never let on. Yet there was something in his eye when he looked at me. Something familiar, protective. I'd felt an attachment to him the first moment we'd met, but I hadn't known why.

"He is indeed your grandfather. He knows it, too. When he learned of the pregnancy, he followed me here, you see. He wanted to stay with me, to raise our child. To marry me. He is such a good man, and noble, too."

"You said no?" I asked.

"Of course I did."

"But why?"

Instead of answering right away, my grandmother walked over to a nearby cupboard, pulled out two cups and saucers, and set them down on the table in front of me.

"Because I loved him too much to let him wither in front of my eyes."

"What do you mean?"

"He was never meant to stay here. He began to age quickly in this place. A year, over the course of days. Then two years over an hour, and so it accelerated. I could see it happening—his hair turning gray, his back beginning to hunch. I couldn't bear the thought that I was stealing time from him. I was stealing his life."

"Is that what happens to everyone who leaves the Other-where?" I asked. I hardly dared think of Callum ever following me to Fairhaven to be with me. But if he did, I couldn't bear the thought of him aging so quickly and possibly dying so soon.

Nana shook her head. "I don't know. All I knew was that I couldn't stay in the Otherwhere and raise his baby, as the Academy would have expelled him. And he couldn't stay here. So he stayed just long enough to grow old with me even as I stayed young, and then we said goodbye. When he went back, he told them he'd tried to persuade me to tell him who the father was, but to no avail. They were shocked by his rapid aging, but it seems they were willing to overlook it, as they made him head of the Academy. The good news, I suppose, is that it sounds like he's stabilized over the years."

I nodded. "But you saw him again, right? He told me he saw you a few years after you found the Relics."

"Yes, he came to visit just once. I'd met your *other* grandfather by then, and Merriwether saw that we were settling down. He wished me well and left again."

She shot me a focused look. "Well, now that the cat's out of the bag, let's talk about the reason you're really here. You came here looking for my blessing, didn't you?"

"Your blessing?"

"To go after the queen yourself."

I clenched my jaw and stared at my hands, which were tightly locked on the table in front of me. "I guess I did," I said. "But I really just wanted to know who my grandfather was. I wanted to know if there was a chance I was as strong as people say I am. Because right now, I'm feeling pretty weak."

"I suspect, Vega dear, you'll find you're far stronger than anyone ever imagined."

Her words gave me the courage to pull myself to my feet. "Do you think I can get them back? Will and Liv, I mean? Do you think I can save them?"

"I think," Nana said, "that if anyone in this world has a chance of doing exactly that, it's you."

End of Book One

BOOK TWO: SEEKER'S QUEST

If you enjoyed this book, please consider leaving a review on Amazon. Reviews help books' visibility and help authors in many, many ways.

Also: Seeker's World, Book Two: *Seeker's Quest,* is coming soon!

I was alone with no heroic prince racing to save me, no merciful lord to offer me a stay of execution, and only myself to rely on.

I could only hope that this time...
I would be enough.

ALSO BY K. A. RILEY

Seeker's World Series:

Seeker's World

Seeker's Quest

Seeker's Fate

Resistance Trilogy

Recruitment

Render

Rebellion

Emergents Trilogy

Survival

Sacrifice

Synthesis

Transcendent Trilogy *(Coming in 2020)*

Travelers

Transfigured

Terminus

Athena's Law Series

Book One: *Rise of the Inciters*

Book Two: *Into an Unholy Land*

Book Three: *No Man's Land*

For updates on upcoming release dates, Blog entries, and exclusive excerpts from upcoming books and more:

https://karileywrites.org

Printed in Great Britain
by Amazon

74666779R00142